W9-AJT-898

Date: 12/12/14

FIC WHITE
White, Carol.
Sitting pretty /

Sitting Pretty

Short Stories

plus

Bonus Novella

Reptilian

PALM BEACH COUNTY
LIBRARY SYSTEM
3650 SUMMIT BLVD.
WEST PALM BEACH, FL 33406

Sitting Pretty

Carol White

Copyright ©2013 by Carol White.

All rights reserved.

No part of this publication may be reproduced or transmitted in any form or by any means, electronic, mechanical or otherwise, including photocopy, recording, or any information storage or retrieval system now known or to be invented, without permission in writing from the publisher, except by a reviewer who wishes to quote brief passages in connection with a review. Requests for permission should be addressed in writing to the publisher—Limit of Liability/Disclaimer of Warranty: While the publisher and author have used their best efforts in preparing this book, they make no representations or warranties with respect to the accuracy or completeness of the contents of this book and specifically disclaim any implied warranties of merchantability or fitness for a particular purpose.

First published by Dog Ear Publishing
4010 W. 86th Street, Ste H
Indianapolis, IN 46268
www.dogearpublishing.net

ISBN: 978-1-4575-2534-6

Library of Congress Control Number: has been applied for

This book is a work of fiction. Names, characters, places, and incidents either are products of the author's imagination or are used fictitiously. Any resemblance to actual events, locales, or persons, living or dead, is entirely coincidental.

Printed and Bound in the United States of America

Also by Carol White

Hidden Choices
From One Place to Another

For the wonderful children in my life

CONTENTS

Rural Stories

Hers

His

Extras

Rural Stories

MARSHY JENKINS

*M*y three favorite fantasies all began with my husband being dead.

The first scenario entailed coming home and finding him shot through the head. I'd call the police and open the door a short while later to a movie star-looking detective who was the meanest son of a bitch on the force. He'd suspect me for a couple of weeks, in which time we would fall hopelessly in love. Together, we'd catch the real killer. I'd marry my detective, raise a couple of cub scouts, and live happily ever after.

My second fantasy involved a rare tropical disease with no cure that would claim my husband's life, leaving me a young widow forced to go out with the brilliant specialist who had tried to save him. We'd soon discover we were meant to be together and since nothing stood in our way, there'd be a lovely wedding and a honeymoon in Acapulco.

The third fantasy had me walking into the house and discovering a knife stuck in my husband's neck. I'd pull it out realizing too late that my fingerprints were all over the murder weapon. I'd make a phone call to a high-powered attorney who would get me off the hook at the last minute. He'd ask the judge to marry us as soon as I was acquitted.

You might be wondering why I wanted my good-looking hunk of a husband dead. You'd be right up there with the rest of the folks around here who thought Thomas Magrith was the greatest, including my mother. My father ran out on us before I was born and I guess he never looked back. Thomas and I had known each other since grade school and he'd been my boyfriend for just as long. When Thomas was eighteen, he asked Mama if he could formally court me. She said yes with a wink because in those days courtship was just an expression for short engagement. Everyone seemed to think we were right for each other. Everyone, that is, except for Marshall Jenkins, or as we all called him, Marshy.

Marshy had been in school with us, although a few years ahead, and had never gotten along well with Thomas. Thomas said he'd tried to make friends, but Marshy wouldn't even shake hands with him. Marshy told me not to ever marry Thomas; said he was meaner than a rattler and just as dumb. He'd never go into any more of an explanation, so it was easier not to believe him. I think Marshy had an eye out for me himself, and it was a case of simple jealousy.

After Thomas and I were married, I saw that Marshy had been only partially right. Thomas didn't have nothing but mean bones in his body; he was dreadful. He'd once thrown a whole dinner against the dining room wall, just like that scene with Carlo and Connie in "The Godfather," and then shouted for me to clean it up. He had this trick of pummeling me with a bag of oranges that hurt plenty, but never left any black and blue marks. Thomas had read about it in one of his *Soldier of Fortune* magazines, and it worked so well he never had to resort to whipping me with a belt or a hanger that would have left telltale signs of abuse. Whenever I saw a bag of oranges on the kitchen table, I knew I was in for it.

The first time he beat me, I ran home to Mama. She sat me down and said I was a grown woman now and told me to find a way to deal with it. "Cherry, you stay away from him when he's in one of his moods," she warned me. "Don't tell no one else about it," was her motherly advice.

It was no fantasy the day I came home to find my husband with an ax deep in his chest, deader than common road kill. I knew enough not to touch the body and I sidestepped the blood to hold my little Merle Norman compact mirror in front of his mouth to see if he was breathing. I took my first easy breath in years when I discovered he wasn't. There was no handsome cop to call; the only law enforcement officer I knew was Al Chambers, the crossing guard down at the day school.

Old Doc McKenna had operated on Chester Goode's wrong leg so he sure as shooting wouldn't be getting a phone call. But I did ring up the only lawyer I knew—Marshy Jenkins.

Marshy was at the door within ten minutes. He found me in sort of a daze just sitting there on the sofa eating a Peppermint Pattie. When he discovered I hadn't called the police, he did it for me. He figured we'd have a few minutes alone until they arrived.

"Did you do it, Cherry?" he said.

"Of course not, Marshy. Why, you know me better than that." I explained that I came home at six o'clock that evening like I do five nights a week after leaving Sadie-Lil's Decorating and Gift Shop, where I'd been working since I was a junior in high school. Everyone said I had a real nice touch with arranging things, and Sadie-Lil called me her "protégée." She'd sunk a lot of learning into me, and I never let her down.

"Tell me what happened next," Marshy said.

"I shouted out to Thomas like I always do and when he didn't answer, I went straight into the kitchen to put up dinner. After my water was on to boil, I went into the bedroom to get out of my good shoes. I put on these old, beat-up terrycloth scuffs 'cause they're real comfortable even though they don't look so high fashion. The bathroom door was partially closed, and when I pushed it open I saw him all crumpled up in the corner. That's when I called you," I said.

I was about to tell Marshy about my mirror breath check when the police walked in. We hadn't ever bothered locking our doors, and the police asked me later why I hadn't started to since my husband had just been murdered.

Marshy stayed with me the whole time the police questioned me down at headquarters. Nothing like this had ever happened in our town and they weren't exactly prepared for an interrogation. They sure as hell didn't know how to play good cop, bad cop. Marshy told them either to make an arrest or let me go. They knew they had to release me, telling me rather dramatically not to leave town, as if I'd had a Swiss chalet to run off to.

Marshy drove me over to Mama's that night because the bathroom in my house needed to get all cleaned up before I could stay there again plus, Inspector Clouseau and his pal had warned me not to go near the crime scene. Marshy and I woke Mama out of a sound sleep to tell her the news about Thomas and, although she knew he wasn't exactly Ward Cleaver, she cried like a baby. I said goodnight to Marshy, not forgetting to thank him for all he'd done, and he promised to check in on me the next morning.

The police tried to build a case against me, but the district attorney said there was no physical evidence except an ax wiped clean of fingerprints, there being no DNA in those days, and more importantly, no motive. Thomas and I were known as a happy couple; honeymooners even after six years of marriage.

All the workers down at the plant said he was always bragging on his sweet little Cherry; how she'd fixed up the house real fancy and loved to cook this special stuffed meatloaf every Friday night for him. Why would a devoted wife like that want to kill her husband? Thomas had even told them we were planning on having a baby soon because we had to stop acting like puppy-love kind of teenagers. So, by the end of the summer when all the kids were back in school, the D.A. stopped his investigation and the police went back to racing their cars on an old dirt strip down by the high school.

That Thanksgiving Mama suggested we have our meal out in a restaurant. She'd read where it was good for people who'd had stressful changes in their lives to do something different for the holidays. I tried to tell her that such advice was for people who were actually grieving, not relieved, happy ones, but she insisted. Mama didn't want to cook a big meal for just the two of us. At the last minute, Marshy called and accepted my invitation for him to join us at The Copper Kettle on Thanksgiving Day.

All three of us ordered the Turkey Day Special, but the meat was dry as burnt toast even though it had been drowned in canned brown gravy. No one could top Mama's turkeys; she farmed them herself and always chose the plumpest ones for holiday dinners. She boasted that her birds had breasts like Marilyn Monroe. Thomas always said that he'd wished I did too as I'd smile behind gritted teeth. Mama's cornbread dressing and sweet potato pie were better than anything The Copper Kettle served, and although she knew to leave the oranges out of the cranberry compote, it was still the best in the county.

"Mama, this meal can't compare to your cooking," I said. "Why don't we put on our regular Christmas spread this year and maybe Marshy will join us. How 'bout it?" Mama hesitated long enough to give him time to accept and offer to bring a special wine that he said went well with turkey.

The next few weeks flew by and I found myself with another one of my fantasies: Marshy, Mama, and I having our first home-cooked dinner together with no fights before, during, or after. This was no instant falling in love and getting married fantasy, so I guess you could say it was more of an expectation.

Mama was as nervous as a mouse looking down a snake's jaw, and nothing I could say would calm her. "Mama, you've done these dinners for lots of holidays. This time's no different except that I don't expect Marshy's going to beat me afterwards."

"I don't know why I'm not up to it this year," Mama said, dragging out her words, "maybe I'll go ahead and buy one of those new frozen self-baster turkeys."

At that moment I knew that Mama had killed Thomas. Wearing thick rubber gloves, Mama had butchered her own turkeys from the time I could remember, with me running away from the bloody event. Now she was mumbling something about her good ax being broken, and not having the time to replace it. I sank down onto Mama's burgundy velvet love seat, and asked her to fix us some iced tea and maybe a plate of Social Teas. Mama nodded like she knew what was coming. A few minutes later, she sat down next to me and both of us sipped, nibbled on cookies, and thought a bit.

"Cherry, I had to do it," Mama said. "I saw you trapped in a marriage that you'd never get out of. I knew he'd beat you if you got pregnant and he'd beat you if you didn't. I couldn't stand by and watch my daughter have a life like that. I didn't know what else to do, so you better go ahead and call the police."

I knew what I had to do. I picked up the phone and dialed a familiar number.

"Hey Marshy, it's Cherry. Just a quick question. Does that wine you're bringing over Christmas day go with ham?"

THE AWFULEST THING
I EVER DONE

I don't come from one of those families where everyone brags about being brilliant and creative. In our family, the most original thing anyone ever did was to drive in reverse down Front Street. Our Cousins' Club thirteenth reunion received a mention in the society section of the local newspaper, but I was mostly known for the time I beat up Cuffy Burton. No, that wasn't the awfulest thing I ever did; that turned out to be about the best. Let me back up a bit so you don't get too confused.

My name is Marcella Green, but from the time I was in the third grade my friends called me Greenie. Mommy and Pap didn't much like it, and they never called me by anything except my given name. I wanted a sister or brother, but Pap said I'd already cost him a bundle and he didn't want to be working past the age of a hundred. Pap was the foreman down at the mill, so I didn't grow up poor like some of the kids did, we usually had enough to put in the church collection box on Sunday and a nice dinner with a roast afterward.

Mommy wanted me to act proper and ladylike. Although I might have considered it, like most kids my age I didn't want to admit that parents could be right about anything. Pap was real sweet. He wasn't much of a disciplinarian, although we had our own little games to fool Mommy. Whenever I was caught doing something wrong, Pap would take me into my room with a rolled up newspaper and swat the wall like crazy while I pretended to cry. When Mommy finally heard enough of this abuse she'd yell out, "That's it, Lester, leave her be now." My guess is that Mommy knew what was going on, but played along anyhow.

When I was in the fourth grade Mommy decided it was time for me to have a library card. She was real friendly with the children's librarian, Miss Grace, who'd told Mommy that my grammar was atrocious and would never get any better if I continued hanging out with the ruffians she'd seen me with. I guess Miss Grace meant my two best friends, Rhonda Burton and her twin brother Cuffy.

The three of us had become blood family by poking our fingers with thin sewing needles and then holding hands until the drawn blood seeped into the tiny holes we'd made, bonding us forever. We did everything together, but there was no denying that Rhonda (who'd been named after Rhonda Fleming, the movie actress) and Cuffy (whose real name was Curtis and wasn't named after anyone I'd ever heard of) didn't have even the small advantages our family had. Their mother had abandoned them when the twins were babies, and their daddy, well, the truth is their daddy was drunk more than he was sober.

Mommy wasn't crazy about me playing at Rhonda and Cuffy's house because there was no supervision, as she'd tell Pap every time I insisted upon going over there.

I was intrigued by the Burton's lifestyle; it was so different from my own. They never went to church and dinner was usually a sandwich or whatever casserole a neighbor had dropped off. Mr. Burton was real good looking (I'm sorry to report that his son and daughter were kind of average in that department), and a lot of women in town, even some of Mommy's friends, tried to take him under their wing. A few single ladies had told Mommy that if they could only get their hands on him and make him stop drinking, George Burton would be perfectly suitable husband material—a lump of clay right for the molding. Mommy just told them, "A drinker is a drinker and all the tuna noodle casseroles in the world won't change that."

That's how Mommy was; she had her ideas, and as I used to say, no amount of nothing could change her.

I got through grade school and junior high pretty good, and when I was in my second year of high school Pap sat me down to discuss getting a part-time job. Except for occasionally babysitting the kids next door, I'd done nothing on a regular basis and was excited over the prospect of having my own money. I'd be able to afford going to the movies with Rhonda and Cuffy every weekend and even treating us to our own popcorn and Dr. Peppers, so's we wouldn't have to split the way we normally did. Pap broke into my millionaire's dream by saying that except for five dollars a week, whatever salary I earned had to go into my college fund.

"What college fund, Pap? I never heard you say nothing 'bout college before," I'd said. "Why start in with that business now? You and Mommy never went and we're doing okay. Mommy even told me we're going out to that fancy new steak house after church this Sunday. You don't need no college education to do that."

"You're right, Marcella, but apparently you do need it to stop saying things like 'awfulest' and that 'you don't need no college education.' Your mommy and Miss Grace have spent a lot of time making sure you use the correct grammar you've learned in school, and if you choose not to use it because you're afraid of giving the wrong impression to the twins, then it's clear you need to be at a university if you ever graduate from high school."

That was the longest speech Pap ever gave me, so I knew he and Mommy had already come to their decision about my future. I didn't really mind, but felt strongly that I had to put up more of a fuss so they wouldn't think I was a pushover.

"Well, Mr. Burton don't, I mean doesn't, even give a good Goddamn if Cuffy and Rhonda cut class the way they do!"

"You watch that talk or you'll be grounded till the cows come home."

"Sorry, Pap," I'd said, meaning it. Cussing was a big offense in our household. Mommy wouldn't even let me say the word lousy. It was low-class, according to her.

"Mommy and I have already discussed it. You'll be going to college in a couple of years so make sure you keep those grades up. In the meanwhile, get yourself down to Mr. Halliday at the Cinema Vogue. I hear my pal Mark has a job for you."

I grabbed Pap around the waist and hugged him till he hollered auntie, another one of our father-daughter games. Pap knew my favorite thing in the whole wide world was going to the movies and if you worked at Mr. Halliday's theatre, you got to watch them for free on your time off. I would have cleaned the latrines to get a job there, but as it turned out that wasn't the available position. Mr. Halliday needed a new girl behind the candy counter.

Mommy ironed my good white blouse that I wore with my new gray pleated skirt. Rhonda had shown me how to French braid my hair, so with compliments on how professional I looked going off for my first job interview, I began the quarter-mile walk into town to meet with Mr. Halliday. I guess Pap and Mommy were about the best parents a girl my age could have. Now that I was going to be making some spending money—even if it was only five dollars a week—I couldn't have been happier.

Mr. Halliday hired me on the spot and showed me around the candy counter. Rows of neatly stacked Dots, Raisinets, M & M's, Jawbreakers, Turkish Taffy, and Clark Bars were ready for the picking by hungry movie-goers. The candy cost ten cents each plus a penny tax and popcorn was fifteen cents. I'm telling you right now that after two weeks on the job I would advise against ever ordering the buttered popcorn unless they've changed the recipe. The butter was a tub of sour-smelling, yellowish shortening type of slush that was melted and re-melted for every shift at the counter. The kids loved it, always telling me to give them two pumps, which I gladly did, as long as I didn't have to eat it myself.

Not ever having much of a sweet tooth, most of the stuff behind the counter didn't appeal to me, plus I was not in the mood to hear Mommy lecture me about how my teeth were going to fall out one day if I ate that junk. I'd never even had a cavity as she well knew, but I guess all mothers feel they have to give out advice on just about everything. No, the candy didn't tempt me, but the ice cream bon-bons sure did. The brand Mr.

Halliday sold came six pieces to a long cardboard box and because they cost a quarter, I usually only sold them to grownups.

Mr. Halliday had said that if I wanted anything from behind the counter, I'd have to pay for it like everyone else who worked at the Vogue. He was sort of cheap; I felt he could have let me take one box of bon-bons for free every so often.

Since most of my friends had part-time jobs it wasn't a big deal for me to be working; that is, except to Cuffy Burton. Cuffy's muddy-brown eyes turned Prell-green with envy when he heard Mr. Halliday had hired me. He had applied for the same job, but because Pap and Mr. Halliday played Pinochle every Tuesday night, let's just say I had an edge. Rhonda was real happy for me, particularly since I was able to sneak her into the Saturday matinees. The two ushers, who were both named Raymond, didn't care, and Mr. Halliday was usually up in his office most likely counting his money. Cuffy, who could have gotten into the shows just as easily, refused to join us. He wanted nothing to do with me, and that's how it stayed for two more years.

I kept my job all through high school and the next time Cuffy spoke to me was at my Sweet Sixteen birthday party that Mommy and Pap had arranged at Ming's, the only Chinese restaurant in town. There were about thirty of us kids down in Mr. Ming's party room, eating tiny eggrolls and dancing to the forty-fives that my friend, Kevin Wright, spun on the record player he'd brought along. Mommy had arranged for Mrs. Ming to serve us Singapore Slings, which was really chilled pineapple juice in tall glasses topped with Maraschino cherries and paper umbrellas. It was the talk-of-the-town kind of party until Cuffy showed up. Cuffy had turned out to be a big, strong boy by the time he was sixteen, and although he'd been invited along with Rhonda, I didn't expect for him to show up. I certainly didn't expect for him to show up drunk.

"Hey, Greenie," Cuffie said, his voice slurring, "or do I have to call you Marcella now that you've got some titties!"

The whole room quieted down even though Kevin had "Hound Dog" blasting on the record player. My parents had told us they wouldn't hang around during the evening having made previous arrangements to go to the movies (compliments of Mr. Halliday, for a change) and would be heading to The Cup Café afterwards. The Mings were busy upstairs serving dinner to the Saturday night crowd, so I found myself in charge.

"Cuffy, if you're drunk, you'd better leave now," I'd said.

Kevin left his post to back me up saying, "That's right, Cuff, it's time for you to go." A few other boys came over to show support for Kevin, who was half Cuffy's size. But it wasn't until Rhonda, who'd grown up pretty big herself, came over and grabbed her twin by the arm and said, "What in the hell do you think you're doing?" that Cuffy turned and raced up the steps into the blackness of night. The party got back to as normal as it could be and I never did tell Mommy or Pap about the intrusion.

Cuffy started hanging around the Vogue and it seemed he was always there when my shift was about over. I'd be taking out the garbage and all of a sudden Cuffy would appear, not saying anything, just leering at me with mean eyes all squeezed up in his puffy face. I did my best to ignore him until the day we came face to face, so to speak. I had decided to throw away the leftover butter, against Mr. Halliday's golden rule, and was about to remove the cover of the garbage can when I felt a pair of brawny arms lift me off the ground.

I knew it had to be Cuffy. Without thinking, I backhanded the open container of rancid sludge into his face with a move that surprised us both. He started screaming that I'd blinded him, and with that I turned and gave him a kick in the place where Mommy had instructed me to if a man ever went for me. Now Cuffy was really hollering, which brought Mr. Halliday outside to see what all the fuss was about.

"Children, children, what is going on out here?" he'd said. "And Marcella, what in the world are you doing with that tub of butter? Why it's half full."

Before I could answer, along came Miss Grace with a bunch of her friends who'd heard the commotion the whole time they'd been at the box office buying tickets for the evening's double feature.

"Mark, why don't you let me take care of this? You go back inside and finish up whatever it is you were doing," Miss Grace said. She'd sized up the situation pretty quickly and Mr. Halliday looked relieved that someone else was going to handle it.

"Okay, Grace, if you think you can get these hooligans to stop fighting. I'll be in my office, Marcella, come up for your paycheck later on. And that tub of butter will be coming out of your salary."

"Yes sir, Mr. Halliday," I'd answered, as polite as I'd ever been.

"Curtis, Marcella, I don't know exactly what went on here, but if the two of you can shake hands and be friends again we won't have to take this any further."

"Yes, Miss Grace," we'd both answered. I extended my hand to Cuffy and we both started crying.

"I have to get back to my counter. Thanks, Miss Grace. See ya, Cuffy."

"See ya, Greenie."

Like I said, that fight with Cuffy was the best thing that ever occurred because I didn't much care for being enemies with my blood brother. We went back to being friends again like nothing had ever happened.

Somebody must have said something to Mr. Burton because later that day he cleaned himself up and marched over to the library to pay a personal call on Miss Grace. Apparently she'd told him that Cuffy and I had had a little scuffle, like all kids do, but it was nothing to be alarmed about. Well, didn't the two of them just hit it off because he asked if she'd like to go out and get supper with him at the diner. Miss Grace agreed on the condition that Cuffy and Rhonda came along. He said that was fine with him and they had their first meal together as the family they eventually would become.

After high school I went off to our state university and majored in drama. Kevin, who became a songwriter, and I were married two years after graduation and settled about ten miles from Mommy and Pap. Kevin and I opened up the first dinner theater in our county and hired Pap as the box office manager after he retired from the mill. Rhonda and Cuffy still live in town with their families and they're always welcome at our opening nights.

Oh, I almost forgot. The awfulest, or the most awful, thing I ever did was to open some of those bon-bon cardboard boxes at the Vogue, and eat one of the six pieces when no one was around. The thing about folks at the movies who bought those bon-bons was that they were never sure if they were on their fifth or sixth piece, and if they thought they were being shorted—well, they never mentioned it to me!

THE RED TILE FLOOR

*M*y father left us on Christmas Eve. Although moving west had been his idea, he was heading back to Richmond, Virginia to be with another family. While Mother wrapped our gifts and stuffed stockings, Father packed his suitcases and said good bye. Mother told us the long days in Montana had been too hard on a professional man, an insurance agent, who wanted clients other than ranchers and the occasional old codger whose policies had run out. My sister, Melanie, and I begged her to fight for him, but she wouldn't have any part of it. "Lila," she said, "change often results in a more rewarding future."

As an eighth grader, I didn't need, nor did I want, change. It was the sixties and extended families weren't as prevalent as they are today.

Two weeks after he left, Melanie and I came home one afternoon to discover a stack of red vinyl tiles in the pantry. Mother had decided to redo the kitchen floor to celebrate her recently acquired independence. That night, after Melanie and I had gone to sleep, Mother peeled the paper off each sticky back tile and applied them neatly on top of the ancient tan linoleum floor.

Father's checks arrived on time each month and Mother used the first one to purchase a secondhand piano for us. With part of the next check she let us get our hair permed and our ears pierced—a ladies day out as Mother called it. She drove us down to Marna-Rae's Salon where the owners, Marna and Rae, wound our hair section by little section around skinny pink rods and squeezed a smelly solution over all of it. They rolled cotton around our heads, wrapped us in plastic caps, and sat us under two hooded dryers making Melanie and me look like a couple of town ladies getting ready for a bridge party. Marna gave Mother a Henna rinse that turned her light brown hair a peculiar shade of mahogany, but Melanie and I told her she looked like an elegant French lady.

We left Marna-Rae's a mass of tight ringlets and headed downtown to Maynard's Jewelry House, where they'd pierce your ears for free if you bought your earrings there. Mrs. Maynard used a special freezing spray so it wouldn't hurt too much, but we were willing to disregard any pain since Melanie and I had been begging to have our ears pierced forever. When Father was still the head of our household he'd forbidden us to do so, saying that we would look like a couple of floozies. We didn't know what floozies looked like, but thought they must be quite lovely if they all had pierced ears.

Melanie wanted golden ball earrings like her friends had, but a pair of tiny sapphire studs, my birthstone, bedazzled me. Mother joked that she didn't see why we couldn't celebrate my September birthday a little early. After we left Maynard's, Melanie and I sprinted down the street while admiring our reflections in the store display windows we passed along the way to Doc's Drugstore. Mother said she was treating us to banana splits even though it was almost dinnertime. I began to think that maybe she was right; some changes weren't so bad after all.

In the springtime, Mother announced she'd taken a job at the All-Day All-Night Diner out on the highway. She tried on her uniform for Melanie and me, and it was so frilly we told her she looked like one of those fancy lamb chops all dressed up in ruffles for Easter dinner. Mother had opted for the breakfast and lunchtime shift, so she could be home in time to greet us when we walked in the house from school. My sister and I insisted we were old enough to take care of ourselves, which meant that we wanted to watch the Mickey Mouse Club and, later on, American Bandstand undisturbed without Mother constantly nagging us about piano practice. Nevertheless, there she would stand, in her kitchen with the red tile floor, pouring milk for us and dispensing Oreo cookies, two by two.

Neither Melanie nor I were musically inclined, but to Mother's ears the two of us were about ready for Carnegie Hall. We took lessons from the high school music teacher, Mr. Hoyt, who came to our house once a week wearing a natty tweed sports jacket and a paisley bow tie. Sometimes, Mother invited Mr. Hoyt to stay for dinner. You'd have thought he hadn't eaten in a month the way he vacuumed up Mother's meals that if they weren't brought home from the diner, would have been one of her tasteless stews topped off with an assortment of dried-up spices.

On the diner nights, as we called them, Mr. Hoyt was likely to find a platter of fried chicken with buttered noodles and freshly baked rolls. Mother tried to bring home cup-custards, because she knew it was our favorite, and you could count on Mr. Hoyt eating at least two of those for dessert. We begged Mother not to ever marry him, but she laughed and said that even if he were the marrying kind, it wouldn't be to her.

One afternoon we came home to find two stray kittens that Mother had taken home from the back of the diner. We named them Minnie and Mickey and set up their bed in the mud room, although they crept into our bedroom from the very first night. Father had been allergic to animals and, according to him, the subject of owning a pet was an open and shut case.

In early May, Mother took us to the garden nursery where we bought flats of colorful flowers to electrify the white garden Father had always taken so much pride in. Then Melanie and I headed down to the river to collect flat, smooth stones that became paths leading nowhere in our new rainbow backyard. As the weather grew warmer, the three of us would sit around on rusted metal chairs amid our vibrant creation and sip lemonade while keeping cool with homemade paper fans. Mother would take off the elastic stockings she'd started to wear at the diner, and put her feet up on an old tree trunk.

My sister and I began to receive letters along with birthday cards and gifts from our father. Mother said it was up to us whether or not we wanted to have a relationship with him. He'd apologized to her a long time ago and now expressed his regrets to us. He was sorry for the way he'd handled things years ago and hoped we could reconnect one day. After a few more letters and several long distance phone calls, he asked Mother if she'd allow us to visit him. She agreed and Melanie and I made our first trip to visit our father, his wife, and her son.

When it came time for Melanie and me to attend college, Mother insisted that Father pay for the best universities we could get into. His business had done well and he was happy to comply. Melanie was accepted at Northwestern and went on to become a pediatric psychologist. I chose Columbia University where I majored in photojournalism. Upon my graduation, I remained in New York, and Melanie settled in Chicago.

My sister and I both stay in touch with Dad, as he insists we call him, and join him and his family every Thanksgiving.

Wherever Melanie and I and our husbands happen to be in December, we return to Montana for Christmas week to celebrate what we call a special Mother's Day. Mother insists on cooking dinner, having long ago retired from the diner. We sit in the kitchen with the red tile floor and eat every last drop of whatever stew she's prepared, telling her that Mr. Hoyt doesn't know what he's missing.

Hers

CLAUDIO'S GARDEN

When Guy Haines asked for my hand in marriage over dinner at the Four Seasons, it was more of a statement than a proposal. The senior partners in his commercial real estate firm were pressuring him to upgrade his single status. Since we loved each other anyway, why not make it official? Who could argue with such logic, especially when he presented me with a five carat pear-shaped diamond flanked by baguettes almost as big as real pears. Guy was one of those successful young Turks who'd done well enough for us to live in his six room penthouse apartment overlooking Central Park.

"Oh, and by the way, Annie," my new fiancé said, "I'm having a painter come up here tomorrow. One of the partners recommended this fellow, Claudio, and says everyone in the firm has used him. Claudio owes Barry a favor and he had a cancellation this week, so he'll take us instead. He'll be here in the morning right after I leave."

I groaned inwardly thinking about the deadline for my story on Santa Fe. I was a travel writer and worked from home, a situation Guy often took advantage of. "Annie," Guy murmured, "you really look special tonight. I love your hair that way."

I had gone to a salon earlier in the day where they teased my long, overly highlighted blond hair into a French twist, which added two inches to my tiny five-foot frame. When I first met Guy he suggested that wearing stilettos would give me the stature he obviously thought I lacked. He also liked me in tight bright clothing, which wasn't exactly my style, but one weekend we ended up on Fifth Avenue where he selected a new wardrobe for me. When I told him I felt like a Barbie Doll all he said was, "What's your point?" I gave in to these guilty pleasures because Guy was a perfect boyfriend in many ways. Charming, good-looking, adventurous (when time allowed, which was almost never), and my parents approved of him. No one approved of my last boyfriend, who was only adventurous and not in a good way.

The next morning I opened the door for Claudio, an attractive man neatly dressed in jeans and a white shirt. I showed him around the apartment and when we walked into the master bedroom, he spotted my shoes from the previous evening.

"Wow, you don't wear those weapons, do you?" he said, pointing to my Jimmy Choo's.

"Yes. Is that a problem for you?" I said, sounding like a mousetrap snapping shut.

"Not for me, but some short women end up looking like Petunia Pig when they wear heels that high. It certainly doesn't fool anyone into thinking they're tall."

If Guy was thrilled with the extra four or five inches these shoes added to my height, who was a painter to compare me to Petunia Pig—and when was the last time anyone had even heard of or seen her? My work had been interrupted and with this insulting comment, I'd had it.

"Claudio, why don't we give you a call later on in the week. I need to get back to work."

"That's okay, but if you don't engage me now, I'll have to fill the spot with another client. There's a long waiting list and I only did this to accommodate someone in your fiancé's firm. I take it you're engaged judging from that rock you're wearing. Don't you think it overwhelms you a bit?"

"Well, I'll have to check to see what size ring Porky gave to Petunia," I said, trying to add a little comic relief to our conversation.

We went back to the living room and studied one white paint chip after another until they all started to look alike.

"Annie, your apartment is very modern, almost stark, and I think this shade of Antique White would soften things up. How do you feel about it?" he asked, holding up a larger swatch.

"I'm not great with fifty shades of white, but your reputation precedes you, so Antique White it is," I said, with a touch of levity that went unnoticed. I had to keep my sarcasm in check because Claudio was right; if I didn't hire him today, Guy would hit the unpainted ceiling.

"Fine, then I'll get all the materials and begin tomorrow morning," he said, ignoring my fifty shades reference. "I work alone, and room by room, so you won't be disturbed too much. It takes longer that way, but my clients seem to prefer it. An apartment this large will take about three weeks."

"Three weeks?" I said. "You can't be serious. How am I supposed to get any work done?"

"We'll leave your office till last; you'll hardly know I'm here."

I called Guy the minute Claudio left and filled him in on the painter with an attitude and no sense of humor. He laughed and said, "Chill Annie, you don't have to marry him; just let him paint the apartment. Don't forget about tonight and wear something sexy. We're meeting the head honchos for dinner and I want you to show off that ring and your body. Make those old geezers jealous. Later, babe."

My plans to rewrite the Santa Fe article were dashed because I'd have to run to the salon for a blow-out, and thoughts about ordering up a pizza for dinner evaporated into thin air. Later on, before pouring myself into another tight outfit, a feeling of unease came over me. I chalked it up to the disruption that the painting would bring and decided to wear my red leather miniskirt (the one Guy asked me to shorten) with a black fitted sweater. I was fastening my killer-high strappy sandals when Claudio's words came back to haunt me. I saw an overdressed cartoon character in the mirror and changed into a pair of black flats at the last minute.

Guy met me at the restaurant and one look told me he wasn't happy with my appearance.

"What happened to the heels, Annie?" he said, hissing like a snake. "You look like a shrimp! And you're late. Ames is already here. How do you think it looks for the boss to be waiting for my girlfriend to show up?"

"I'm your fiancée, darling, and if he's drunk as usual, he won't even have noticed. Come on, let's go and sit down," I said, standing on my tiptoes to plant a kiss on his cheek.

I made a big deal of how I got stuck in traffic and then Guy announced our engagement. The women complimented my ring, which immediately cheered up my sulking fiancé, but the rest of the evening read like a bad script. When the conversation wasn't about business, it turned toward weekend homes in the Hamptons, the latest sports cars, and anything else they could one-up each other on.

"I hear you were lucky enough to get Claudio," said Jemima Ames, the boss's wife, who was nipped, tucked, lipo'd, and Botoxed to perfection. "How about that gorgeous black curly hair of his?"

"I hadn't noticed," I said, although I had. "He didn't stay long." Just long enough to irritate me for the rest of the afternoon.

The next morning after Guy left, Claudio arrived and began moving furniture into the middle of the living room, so he could start the wall preparation. True to his word, I wouldn't have known he was in the apartment until he knocked on my office door around noon.

"Is there a decent place around here for a sandwich?" he said. "I usually bring something with me, but I didn't want to be late on my first day, teacher."

So he did have a sense of humor.

"You could try Ernie's. It's around the corner."

"How about joining me? I feel bad that we kind of got off on the wrong foot. Are you hungry?"

I had skipped breakfast and was starving.

"As long as we don't take too much time," I said, closing down my screen.

Once inside the luncheonette we were seated at a window table, and chatted amiably until a waitress I hadn't seen before brought us menus.

"Hi, my name's Tippi and I'll be, oh my god, will you look at that diamond," she said. "Congratulations, you guys. I'll bring you some water while you decide although I recommend Ernie's special, the pulled pork sandwiches. The sauce is on the table."

I started to explain that Claudio wasn't my fiancé, but she'd already taken off for the kitchen.

"Annie, were you embarrassed that she thought you were engaged to a painter?" Claudio said, with a chuckle.

"Of course not," I said, protesting hard. "Guy and I come in here all the time and now she's got the wrong impression." But he'd been right. I didn't want her to think that I was going to marry a workman in white overalls.

"Annie! Look at this," he said, showing me a bottle of sauce on the table. "It's Dimples Barbeque Sauce—Dimples! Just like yours. We have to order the special now that there's a sauce named after you," he said, as I gave him a big smile showing off what he'd just teased me about.

Claudio scraped and painted for the next few weeks while I put the finishing touches on my Santa Fe story. He and I began having lunch together in the kitchen, neither of us wanting to spare the time to go out.

"One of these days I'm going to learn how to cook, so I could offer you a decent meal once in a while," I said, while munching on the sandwich I'd thrown together.

Claudio was always polite and never mentioned my stilettos or the diamond ring again, but I was still uneasy. Here I was talking and laughing with a contractor in the intimate kitchen space, wondering why Guy wasn't sitting across from me. My fiancé and I were on a treadmill of either dining out with his partners or going to their homes for elaborate dinner parties. We hadn't eaten home in a month.

The next afternoon as Claudio was ready to leave, he asked me to come down to Chelsea the following morning.

"There's an apartment I want you to see, a loft really. The walls are done in a finish that would be perfect for your office. I don't think we should use white in there; it doesn't suit you. Can you get downtown by eleven?"

My article was finished and submitted and I couldn't think of a reason to say no. He wrote down the address, and we made plans to meet in front of the building.

The next day dawned as one of those sparkling fall New York mornings and I found myself looking forward to meeting Claudio. As my taxi pulled up to the address, he hurried over to pay the fare.

"You don't have to do that," I said, secretly pleased that he was acting like such a gentleman.

"Let's go see the apartment. I have the key," he said.

He and I entered the first floor loft that had an open kitchen, an airy living room and a sleeping alcove partially hidden by a bamboo screen. The walls had a slight crackle finish to them and were painted a delicate shade of butterscotch. Claudio was right; it would be ideal for my office.

"I never would have thought of this color, but it's wonderful. It's so soothing," I said, looking around the roomy loft. "What a great apartment except for those horrendous paintings ruining your beautiful walls. How in the world could they have hung that stuff? It must kill you."

"They're pretty bad, but forget about that for now. As long as we're here, let me show you the patio. The owner won't mind."

When we stepped outside to a garden filled with flowers and greenery, I instinctively knew this was Claudio's home.

"Yeah, I'm the owner," he said, reading my mind.

"Why didn't you tell me?" I said. "And you painted those pictures, didn't you? I'm so embarrassed. Please forgive me."

"It's okay, no one else likes them either; that's why I became a house painter to make a living. Come on, let's have lunch outside, I owe you for all those meals you were going to cook for me."

He'd made a *Torta Rustica*, a country tart, that when cut into became a brilliant mosaic of colors and textures. Claudio and I ate at a tiny café-style table and while he poured red wine into glass tumblers, we smiled and continued our conversation. After lunch, he suggested a visit to an art gallery owned by his neighbor where there was an endless supply of espresso. Our hands accidentally touched as we walked the long sunlit blocks of Chelsea to Artistic Abstracts and I was glad I'd forgotten to wear my ring.

"Claudio, how nice to see you," said Gillian, as she kissed him on both cheeks.

"This is Annie Morton, the client I told you about. Annie, Gillian Holroyd," he said. "I promised her some of your famous espresso."

"So nice to meet you. I've heard quite a bit about you," she said, "let me get the coffee started."

While Gillian was in the kitchen I decided to do a little detective work.

"And what exactly have you been telling Gillian about your client?"

"I'm sorry I introduced you like that. We're friends, right?" he said, embarrassed.

I nodded, but wasn't quite sure how to consider the man I'd only known for a few weeks.

"Gillian's been generous to me. She's even taken some of my artwork on consignment. Occasionally she hoodwinks an uptown designer into buying a piece, but mostly it just sits here." Claudio said with a smile, as he pointed to a garish orange and gold canvas.

"Oh, don't be so hard on yourself," Gillian said, hearing our conversation on her way back from the kitchen. "I told you I've seen much worse, and some of those top-notch decorators wouldn't know a good painting if it fell on top of them. They only come in here because they think Chelsea is still one of the latest art oases."

We left the gallery later that afternoon in a grayish twilight and I knew I'd be late getting home.

"Annie, don't marry Guy," Claudio said. "You can't possibly be satisfied with that kind of life. Give us a chance. Don't you see how right we are for each other?"

I remember thinking, "Is this guy crazy?" right before he kissed me.

I left the engagement ring and all (well, most) of my high heels in the penthouse with a note telling Guy I'd call him with an explanation. I moved the rest of my things into Gillian's guest room.

True love is sharing your life with a person you want to grow old with, when diamond rings and fancy dinners have lost all their meaning. It's a simple gold band you exchange with your husband on your wedding day and, maybe if you're lucky enough, your marriage will take place in a Chelsea garden surrounded by family, friends, and a delicious *Torta Rustica*.

FLORAL ARRANGEMENTS

I'm tidying up the living room because my boyfriend Brent is coming over any minute with something very important to discuss with me. I'm sure it's a marriage proposal with plans for a honeymoon in Paris. That's been my dream forever. Tonight's the night; one taste of my *coq au vin*, and one gander at these leggings and lace cami, and it's a done deal.

When the doorbell rings I call out, "Brent, honey! Are you finally here for our special evening?"

"Uh, no, it's not Brent. Brent sent me because he said he's running late."

"Who are you, and why would Brent send you when he's on his way here?"

"It's a surprise. I can't tell you," says the man on the other side of the door. "I'm kind of doing him a favor; could you please open the door."

This conversation is going nowhere, so I kick it up a notch.

"If you don't tell me what the surprise is, I'll call the police."

"Hold on, let me explain. Your name is Georgia and Brent is your boyfriend, and he's running late because he's on his way to a travel agency, so I said I'd deliver these myself," he continues, all in one breath before sealing the deal with something only Brent could have told him. "You're making *coq au vin* because that's his favorite dish, right? He called it 'winey chicken,' but I prefer the correct name."

"Deliver what?" I ask, impressed that he knows the French version for the casserole that Brent put in a request for. I open the door to a ginormous floral arrangement with a pair of lime green eyes peeking out from over the hydrangeas.

"Surprise!" he says, handing me the flowers.

Surprised? I'm totally shocked because Brent's never been the extravagant type and this bouquet must have cost a fortune. I adjust my cami—no use looking sexy for the delivery guy.

"Wow," I say, "Brent picked these out?"

"He came into the shop to order the flowers and when he gave me your name I realized I knew who you were," says the delivery man who without the flowers in front of his face, is seriously cute. "Brent picked out six carnations, but I knew that wasn't right, so I put these together. He'll think I made a mistake with the arrangement. We don't make deliveries for such small orders, but I was on my way home and said I'd do it for him."

"Well, Brent isn't exactly the romantic type...he's more practical. This is such a change from his usual behavior and that's why this evening has to be perfect," I say, although I'm a little miffed that my intended thought a half-dozen carnations would be the right touch for a romantic evening. Brent must be saving for our trip to Paris. We were supposed to go a few months ago, but something came up and he had to cancel. He's probably picking up brochures at the travel agency right now.

I almost sigh daydreaming about the evening ahead, but the delivery guy already thinks I'm paranoid and I don't want to add lovesick to the mix.

"Like I said, Brent's very practical, but he's also smart and funny, and handsome, like one of those guys on Mad Men. And he always tells me how understanding I am...and he loves my cooking," I say, rationalizing his stingy floral purchase.

"Hey, you don't have to sell me. You're the one who has to like him," he says, before adding, "I have to admit, he did seem pretty excited about tonight."

"Of course he's excited. He's going to propose and we're going to Paris. Who wouldn't be thrilled?" I say, before coming back down to earth. "Wait a minute; aren't you going to get in trouble for using such expensive flowers? And that vase is gorgeous."

"Nah, it'll be okay with the boss."

"What shop did you say you work at?" I ask.

"*Fleur de Lee*" over on Oak Street. I'm Lee," he says, and we both laugh.

"So you *are* the boss. I've been in your shop many times, but I don't remember seeing you there," I say.

"I work in the back, but I've noticed you," Lee says, with a flirtatious grin. I ignore the remark and his adorable smile and ramble on about how much I love everything French.

"I go to the flower marts in Paris every spring, so I'm pretty familiar with the city," he says. "There's no place like it. Have you ever been?"

"Not yet, but I have a feeling I'll be there soon. I'd love to talk about Paris, but I really need to call Brent because my *coq au vin* is going to dry up if he doesn't get here in the next ten minutes. You might as well help yourself to a glass of wine," I add in a non-committal way even though I'm hooked on the conversation and those insanely green eyes of his. "When Brent gets here you can apologize to him in person for making the wrong delivery—I won't give you away."

"Sure, Georgia. It'll be our little secret," he says, in a familiar way.

I call Brent from the kitchen and when I return, Lee's poured the *Sauvignon Blanc* and offers up a seat next to him on the sofa.

"Nice-looking fabric," he says, stroking one of the cushions before taking a sip of wine.

"Oh, do you like it? I recently had it reupholstered," I say, glad that he noticed the elegant soft blue French toile print.

"You really like French stuff, huh? I noticed the Monet prints in the hall, unless they're the originals, in which case I'll send you the bill for the flowers."

He has a nice laugh and when he crinkles up those eyes he's a cross between Ashton Kutcher and Channing Tatum. I shut down my groupie stare and want to giggle at his joke, but maybe something is beginning to feel wrong.

"Did you reach your boyfriend?" Lee says, reading my mind. "Is he on his way?"

"He's still at the travel agency. He said to read the note card in the meanwhile."

"Oh right, there was a note. Sorry about that," he says, as he pats down his pockets. Before he hands it to me he asks how long Brent and I have been dating.

"Three years."

"Three years and you're still waiting for a ring?"

"Brent isn't quite divorced. Janet, his wife, is taking him through the mill.

Wait, I bet the divorce has finally come through. That's got to be it. He said we'd get engaged and go to Paris when that happened, which explains the flowers and the travel agency. Lee, did he mention anything about a ring? Sometimes guys like to show off that kind of stuff."

"Georgia, trust me, if a guy thinks six carnations is a big deal for a hot night ahead, there's no way he's coming up with a diamond."

"You don't know that; maybe he wants us to pick it out together," I say, back on the defense team. "And I'd much rather have our honeymoon in Paris. Lots of people get engaged today without a ring," I say, hoping that Brent will show up with something to prove Lee wrong.

"Okay, I'll give you that, but if tonight's so special why didn't he invite you out for dinner?"

"Brent says my cooking is better than any restaurant. He eats here during the week," I say.

"What about the weekends? He could take you out then, no?"

"No, because he spends the weekends with his two daughters. At least Janet lets him do that. She's very difficult, and doesn't understand him like I do. I can't wait to be a step-mom. I hope they'll like me," I blurt out.

"You've been going out with Brent for three years and you still haven't met his kids? Georgia, step-children are fine, but what about having your own?"

"Sure I've thought about it, but Brent's ten years older than I am, and he's already told me he's going out of the baby business. Maybe he'll change his mind after we're married," I say, knowing he won't because he's already scheduled a vasectomy next month even though I pleaded with him to reconsider.

What I would normally classify as an interrogation seems more like a sincere conversation with someone I hardly know, but who is way more empathetic than Brent. But I'm marrying Brent and as soon as he gets here it'll all be quite clear to Lee how much my boyfriend loves me. Brent is more business-like. He doesn't have time to be empathetic.

"Georgia, I know we just met but I can't help having this feeling that he's not the right man for you. I would have taken you to this little French bistro right around the corner, even if you are a great cook. I design their floral arrangements, and I bet they'll give us a cozy table if we leave right now. You deserve a night out even if it's not with Burt."

"It's Brent," I say, correcting him.

"It says Burt on his credit card."

"It does? Maybe Brent's his middle name," I counter. "He used a credit card for six carnations?"

"Yes to the credit card, and not even close on the middle name thing, but you haven't given me an answer to my suggestion," he says.

"Lee, please, that's very nice of you, but I can't go to a restaurant when my boyfriend or, I should say, my fiancé will be here any minute. Let me see the note please, and I told you, Brent loves my cooking and of course he's the right man for me. He's just late," I say, protecting the man I'm going to marry.

Lee looks resigned and hands me the note.

"Thanks," I say, softening, "I appreciate your keeping me company; I've been so nervous about tonight," I add, ripping open the envelope, but after the second line, the floodgates open.

"What is it? Lee says, as he takes the note from my shaking hands and reads it aloud.

"Dear Georgia, Might as well get right to the point. Janet and I decided to get back together. Remember the weekend you and I

45

were supposed to go to Paris and I had to cancel? That was a new beginning for Janet and me. I know you'll understand because you're the most understanding woman ever, and the best cook! Sorry to miss dinner, but I had to pick up the tickets. Thanks to you, we're going to Paris. Enjoy the flowers. The guy in the shop offered to deliver them. Hope you gave him a nice tip. Brent P.S. You were right about the vasectomy, I canceled it."

Lee's eyes narrow right before he rips up the paper.

"Please don't cry. I'm sorry you feel bad. Let Janet have him, he doesn't deserve you."

"And you don't deserve to sit here through my hysterics," I say, hoping my mascara isn't running down my face. "And to think I spent hours preparing his 'winey chicken.' I'd like to dump it on his head."

"Or, you could put the *coq au vin* in the fridge, and let me take you to that French bistro for dinner."

I look at the torn bits of the kiss-off letter from Brent/Burt when I realize something.

"If I add a little more wine, *coq au vin* is actually better the next day," I say, wiping away the last tear.

"Fine, we'll have it tomorrow, but tonight it's champagne, and maybe *boeuf bourguignon*, and I'll tell you all about Paris," Lee says, pulling me to my feet.

I whisper the best French word I know. "Merci."

46

CONVENIENT FRIENDSHIPS

eDe Stein and I thought Laurel Gould was the luckiest girl we'd ever known. Along with brains, beauty, and rich parents who adored and spoiled their only child, Laurel considered us to be her closest allies. DeDe and I had been best friends since the seventh grade when her family bought the house two doors down from ours. I was outside one Saturday morning helping my father weed the flowerbed when DeDe passed by walking a scruffy looking mutt.

"Hello there, young lady," my father said, totally embarrassing me. "Welcome to the neighborhood. Met your folks the other night at the block party. Your dad's quite a square dancer. Well, I'll leave you two girls to get acquainted."

"Thanks, Mr. Sharp. Hi, my name's Delia, but everyone calls me DeDe. My mom said I should come over and meet you," said the most exotic looking teenager I'd ever seen. DeDe had a broad face with a smile that showed off her straight white teeth. Her eyes reminded me of our cat's; sort of that yellowish-green color, and her lips, with just a touch of gloss, curved upward. "I'm going to be in your homeroom as of tomorrow."

"Hi," I said, trying not to smile because my mouth was seriously crowded with braces. "I'm Jessie. It's short for Jocelyn, which I hate and no one calls me that except my brother when he wants to bug me."

"Yeah, brothers can be a pain. I have two," said DeDe.

Cradling her dog, DeDe plopped herself down beside me on the ground, and from that moment on we were practically inseparable. The longest we ever went without seeing each other was during her family vacations to visit relatives up in Maine and a few summers she spent in Europe with Laurel and her family. Long before household computers and cell phones made their debut, whenever we were separated she and I wrote daily letters on flowered stationery updating each other on our summertime routine.

Miriam Lefkowitz, who lived across the street, had been my best friend for three or four years before I met DeDe. Miriam was a pleasant doughy kind of a girl who sighed a lot and was more attuned to staying home and reading than going to the beach with me, or participating in any kind of sports. With her strict upbringing, she adhered to her observant Jewish parents' boundaries. My family was also Jewish, although you'd never know it because we didn't go to temple except for my brother's Bar Mitzvah. We celebrated Passover...sometimes.

DeDe was half and half, which only added to her appeal. No one on our block or in the entire neighborhood had any kind of a mixed marriage. DeDe's parents, Joe (Jewish) and Joanne (Christian) Stein, were a real anomaly. They were a good-looking, sophisticated couple with their matching names, long cigarettes, and cut crystal hi-ball glasses, which held an endless stream of scotch that they drank while lounging in their shag-carpeted den with a built-in wet bar. Mrs. Stein prepared dishes like Chicken Cacciatore and Shrimp Newberg, a far cry from my mother's specialties of baked chicken and fried fish fillets.

When Miriam opened her door the day I met DeDe, she saw us rolling around in the grass and playing with the dog as we carried on the kind of giggly conversation only thirteen-year old girls can have without appearing ridiculous. The kind that Miriam and I never had. Miriam walked across the street and gave a heavy sigh before sitting down on the lawn with us. I introduced the two girls, realizing it would end badly. After Miriam extended her hand for a shake that didn't happen, DeDe gave her a brief greeting before flashing a look that clearly meant, "I've moved into your territory."

50

After twenty minutes of Miriam trying to look comfortable with the situation, she went home saying she had to help her mother with Friday night Shabbat dinner. She was sad, but there was nothing I could do to reverse what was happening, and frankly, I was glad to see her leave, for her sake and mine.

"Is that your best friend?" DeDe asked, as soon as Miriam was out of earshot.

"Yeah, well kinda...our families moved here the same time so you know how that goes."

DeDe twisted her lips and narrowed her feline eyes before laying down the law.

"Then we'll be bestest friends."

I often go back to that day regretting that I gave up a true friend for DeDe, but my new pal was so appealing and we made an ideal pair. Both of us were tall and lanky; me with wavy dirty blond hair and DeDe with her straight, shiny brown Dutch boy bob. We looked right together, and when you're in the seventh grade that's what matters.

Over the weekend my mother reminded me about the upcoming Friday night school dance and suggested that I invite DeDe. Mom said it was tough being the new kid coming into school in the middle of the year and for a change I was happy to accommodate her wishes. I'd introduce DeDe to all my friends and make her part of the in crowd, the cool girls club. Miriam had squeaked in mainly due to our close association, but she was always in temple on Friday nights so I knew she wouldn't be at the dance.

I felt guilty about dropping her, but it wasn't intentional. DeDe and I had hit it off so quickly; it was much more than being thrown together the way Miriam and I had been. We were naturally compatible and she never complained or sighed the way Miriam did. DeDe was almost as athletic as I was, and it would only be a matter of time before she made the cheerleading squad. That was only one of the activities we'd end up in together, so it really made sense for us to be best friends.

"Listen, Mom told me to call you about the school dance on Friday. Wanna come with me?" I said to her, during one of our many daily phone calls.

"Oh my god! That is so great. I'll ask my mom, but I'm sure she'll say it's okay," she said. "What are you going to wear? I mean this is my first dance and I don't want to look like a freak or anything."

"Either my red pleated skirt with a white sweater set, or maybe the navy dress my mom bought me. No one gets real fancy. You probably have something," I said, picturing the stylish wardrobe her Christian mother had probably chosen for her at Lord and Taylor's, unlike the navy dress my brother said made me look like a nun.

"Oh, okay. I have a pink skirt with a matching sweater, does that sound about right?" DeDe said.

"Yeah, and if you wear a skirt and sweater, then I will too. I don't even like the dress," I said.

"Thanks, bestest."

After my dad dropped us off at school, we threw our coats over some empty chairs, and I noticed that DeDe had decided to wear a dress after all. It was a Dupioni silk chemise style with a bow at the hipline in the same yellowy-green color as her eyes.

"I guess I went a little overboard with the dress, but Mom wanted me to make a nice impression. My mom isn't cool like yours. Do I look okay?"

I assured her that she looked more than okay, and that my mom was big on first impressions also.

"There's Nicky Rutland," I said, my eyes scanning the gymnasium.

Nicky, who at thirteen was already the class wolf, took one look at DeDe's matching dress/eye combination and fell in love for the first time in his young life. He asked her to dance, and thus began the magic between them.

Knowing his reputation, I tried to talk her out of it, but they went steady all through junior high and high school. Nicky and I had always been buddies, but my initial crush evaporated while watching him work a party or dance. He was Hollywood-handsome and had a dreamy kind of look with eyelashes the girls would have killed for.

Laurel made an appearance at the dance mainly to meet up with DeDe and me. Laurel didn't hang out with our classmates and had zero interest in the immature boys of thirteen or fourteen, but she was a good sport that evening. I even saw her dancing with Jim Diamonte, and laughing with the girls later on over his greasy pompadour.

Laurel Gould lived in a split-level home in the wealthiest section of town. Her family had a kidney-shaped swimming pool, all the rage back then, and she went to sleep-away camp during the summer, neither of which we had or did. She invited DeDe and me to sleep over so many times that my father joked about paying them rent. The three of us would sit at a mirrored dressing table in the master bedroom while Mrs. Gould made us up with pouty lips and doe eyes, and then teased and sprayed our hair into elaborate beehives.

Laurel's mom let us sleep in her big round bed with pink satin sheets while she and her husband shacked up in the guest room. I only say shacked up because they were the most lovey-dovey parents I'd ever seen. They weren't smokers or drinkers like DeDe's folks, but they were always kissing and hugging, humiliating Laurel with their open display of affection, which DeDe and I thought was cute. After dinner, the housekeeper would serve us homemade blueberry pie (I begged my mother to ask for the recipe, but anything more complicated than buying Drake's Cakes was beyond her) and poured milk into frosted glasses before tucking us in.

It wasn't until after our senior year that I found out Laurel had started inviting DeDe for sleepovers without me.

DeDe and Nicky were the perfect couple, but I was his confidant when they fought, when they broke up, and when they reconciled. He was fearful that she'd leave him for someone else because there were times he'd call and she wasn't home or at my house, and he was sure she had another boyfriend. I told him not to worry because she would never keep anything that important from me.

I dated Tony Wendice all though high school, but it wasn't a deep soulful relationship; more like a weekend and prom date. We had heavy make-out sessions, but it never progressed beyond that. DeDe and I had made a pact to save our virginity for our wedding nights. Nicky confided in me, although not to his girlfriend, that he couldn't make the same promise.

DeDe and I both won partial scholarships to the same university and decided on a general liberal arts program that would lead to teaching careers. Nicky, who'd been valedictorian of our class, had been accepted to Yale on a full scholarship and would eventually, after being kicked out twice and losing his award, go on to become a successful wealth management investment advisor.

Laurel, another honor student, had been accepted to Radcliffe. DeDe and I were invited for lunch at her house a few days before she left. As Laurel packed the dozen or so different colored mohair sweaters her mother bought for her, we all said a teary goodbye.

DeDe and I roomed together, and only saw Laurel during the summer, that is, when her parents hadn't swooped her off to Europe. After our freshmen year, the Goulds began to take DeDe along on their trips because Laurel needed someone to spend time with while her parents went off sight-seeing. Although I was invited as well, when Laurel told me how much it would cost, I knew it would have stretched my parents' budget, and any money I made at summer jobs went toward college expenses. I wondered how DeDe's parents, with her dad out of a job half the time, could afford to send their daughter off to Europe for six weeks, but my father, always respectful of other people's money, told me it wasn't my place to pose the question.

During our last year of college, DeDe met a namby-pamby type of boy named Mitch Brenner and decided he might make better husband material than Nicky. After she'd found out about his indiscretions with other women and after he'd been expelled from Yale, she thought twice about a future with him. To top it off, Nicky's roommate Ben had called her one night and said that Nicky had seduced his girlfriend, and that he was moving out of their suite. Nicky admitted to his flings, but denied the allegation about Ben's girlfriend. By then, DeDe had already settled on Mitch.

"Well, Jessie, I guess I should have listened to you back in junior high and never gotten involved with him. And to think I was saving myself for that bastard all these years, and he's been screwing around on me. Please don't say 'I told you so.'"

"Aren't you going to at least give him a chance to explain?" I said, feeling a sudden loyalty to Nicky. "You guys have been together for so long, and you don't know the full story. Maybe Ben got it wrong."

"Nope, Nicky dropped out of Yale for two semesters so he won't be graduating until next spring, and who's gonna hire someone who screws up a full scholarship? Mitch is going to be a CPA and he's already found an internship in New York. In a few more years he'll have a big-time career, and I'll find us one of those fabulous co-ops in the city, maybe with a terrace or a fireplace. That's the kind of man I want to be married to, not some jerk who may or may not graduate from Yale."

DeDe and Mitch married right after graduation, despite my plea that she and I share an apartment in New York for the first year. The Steins went all out (and into hock as I later discovered) for the wedding, and DeDe could have been photographed for Harper's Bazaar. DeDe selected and paid for my maid of honor dress without consulting me. It was an olive green and beige lace monstrosity, which she must have realized would look terrible on me. She swore, as some brides did, that it could be cut down to a beautiful cocktail dress after the wedding. It couldn't, but I wore it anyway. DeDe was still my best friend, and I would have done anything for her. Laurel, who was engaged to a surgeon but came unescorted to the wedding, was a bridesmaid, and DeDe had okay'd the light taupe crepe gown she'd brought back from Paris.

The market was flooded with fresh young accountants looking to join the top Manhattan companies and after a year of interviewing, the best the headhunters could do for Mitch was to place him with a solid firm in Ohio. DeDe and Mitch moved to a suburban community shortly thereafter where she buried herself in women's activities while trying to get pregnant. After months of frustration and two miscarriages, her doctor advised them that DeDe would probably not be able to conceive, and if they wanted a baby, they might consider adoption. Mitch refused, so without anything further to keep her home except taking care of the house and her husband, DeDe was free to visit me occasionally over the years that followed.

I lucked out finding a rent-controlled apartment in Manhattan, got bored teaching jaded fifth graders at a fancy private school, and decided to continue my own education at night. With an MBA in tow, I became a consultant for start-up companies and after paying my dues I did well, but still kept my cheap one-bedroom apartment.

My dating life was spotty because I was spending so much time getting my career off the ground. Nicky, who was still single, and I kept in touch and occasionally met for dinner. Contrary to DeDe's belief, he'd finished first in his undergraduate class, albeit a year late, and went on to graduate school where again he excelled in his studies. DeDe's name rarely came up in our conversations, so I was surprised when he asked for her number.

"Nicky, she's happily married; don't go upsetting the applecart," I said.

"Don't worry, I have a little unfinished business with her," he said, while signaling the server for another bottle of wine.

"I know she was the love of your life and that she hurt you with the break-up, but let it go," I said.

Nicky look confused before answering.

"Love of my life? Jessie, that was a long time ago."

I was surprised at his statement; I was the one who'd romanticized their relationship.

In between clients one day, I happened upon "Evening Laurel," a designer fabric showroom near Bloomingdale's, and spotted Laurel Gould helping a customer. She and I had lost touch after DeDe's wedding, but I instantly recognized her. She caught my eye, and ran to the entrance to greet me. It was a short, but wonderful reunion. Laurel and I realized that we couldn't possibly catch up in the middle of either of our busy days, so she suggested we meet for cocktails that evening. There was much to discuss and I wanted to find out about her surgeon husband after noticing the exquisite Cartier diamond wedding band she wore. I was about to comment on it when an older woman approached and put a protective hand on Laurel's shoulder.

"Well, who do we have here?"

Laurel introduced me to her business partner, Eve Kendall, a dead ringer for Barbara Bel Geddes, at least ten or twelve years our senior, and as I shook her right hand, I noticed a ring that matched Laurel's on her left. It took me all of four seconds to see that they were more than business partners; they were lovers.

Living in Manhattan, I had the occasion to meet many gay people so the realization that Laurel and Eve were lesbians didn't shock or upset me. Thinking back, hadn't I heard through the grapevine that Laurel had broken her engagement to the doctor when he pressed her to set a wedding date?

I expected to hear the entire story during our date for cocktails that evening, only I didn't. Laurel and I discussed business, family, and DeDe. Other than a birthday card now and then, they had lost touch.

"You're in luck," I said. "DeDe's coming to New York next month to spend a week with me. I know she'd love to get together." I didn't mention the other reason DeDe was coming to visit this time. She'd heard from Nicky and stifled in a boring marriage with Mitch, DeDe was curious to see what her old flame had to offer. Nicky hadn't taken my advice nor would DeDe, so I left it up to them to step blindly into their future.

Laurel invited us up to her apartment the day DeDe came to town for cocktails before going out to dinner. I primed DeDe with the information about Laurel and Eve, but she refused to believe it.

"You said she never came right out and told you they were…lesbians, right? And anyway, Laurel has too much to offer a man to waste it on a woman," DeDe said, ignoring my groans.

We walked over to Laurel's that evening and, while on a tour of her elegantly decorated apartment, DeDe couldn't help but notice that even though there were two bedrooms in the spacious residence, there was only one bed. King sized. Eve joined us in the living room for a glass of wine, but declined our half-hearted invitation to come out to dinner with us.

"I'm going to pass, but you girls go and catch up. DeDe, Laurel's already told me some of the crazy times you two had in Europe—mighty generous of her folks to have treated you. I guess back then things weren't quite as expensive as they are now. Well, I've got some soup going in the kitchen and it's just about ready," Eve said, leaving us for her Dutch oven filled with vegetables and broth and leaving me perplexed as to who had paid for what during those European jaunts and why.

When Laurel went in to say goodnight to Eve, DeDe and I saw her lean in over Eve's shoulder to sniff the soup and say, "Smells good, honey, see you later."

At dinner, Laurel revealed that she'd met Eve several years ago and they'd fallen in love. Eve was divorced and had been out of the closet for a long time before they met, yet she waited for Laurel to make the first move.

"Eve told me she had to be sure it was the real thing before I changed my entire life; that it wasn't just a gal crush or some crazy infatuation I had with her. I always knew I wasn't straight even back in high school and later on when I became engaged," Laurel said, looking at DeDe. "I had a few affairs with women, but when I met Eve that was it for me. I was at my parents' country club waiting to join a foursome when the pro ran me out to the first tee. I spotted a beautiful petite woman, in knickers yet, holding on to her driver, and I fell in love. It was that simple. I'd never felt like that with anyone else before. Or since. At the end of the day I told her not to forget about me. You know what she said? 'You're all I'm going to remember.' Hah! What man would ever say that?"

I laughed along with Laurel, but DeDe sat there mute, those cat-like eyes of hers wide open.

Looking straight at DeDe, she said, "Don't look so shocked; it happens to the best of us."

"What did your parents say?" DeDe said, when she found her voice.

"When Eve took me in as a business partner, her firm was already thriving so my parents helped stake me until I earned a salary. But when she and I moved in together, it was a horrible scene. My dad eventually came around, but my mother still thinks it's the biggest mistake I ever made. She was already planning an elaborate wedding because I was engaged at the time Eve and I met. I don't know what upset her more, the fact that I was a lesbian or that she had to cancel the caterer. Eve's kids are wonderful. They've been totally supportive and treat me like one of the family."

In those ten minutes of conversation, every drop of blood drained from DeDe's face. We got through dinner, said goodnight, and DeDe and I grabbed a cab back to my apartment. DeDe started crying in the taxi and didn't stop until she crawled into bed with me for a post mortem.

"Laurel's too beautiful to be having sex with that woman. They're business partners who happen to be sharing an apartment because rents in this city are so crazy high. And did you see that place? My god, it's huge. It's where Mitch and I should be living instead of some crappy ranch house out in nowheresville. And lots of women take roommates," DeDe said, going on with her fantasy.

"DeDe, did you not hear anything Laurel told us? They're in love. They have sex. So shut up, deal with it, and go to sleep. You can stay in bed if you stop that wailing. Otherwise, open the convertible. It's already made up."

"No, I want to stay with you, like we did when we were kids," she said, still sniffling, but eventually turned on her side and fell asleep before I had a chance to grill her on who paid for the European summer trips.

The next evening DeDe planned to meet Nicky for dinner at the Tavern on the Green in Central Park. In a flurry of excitement, she ransacked my closet for something to wear and at seven o'clock in my one good Calvin Klein suit bought on sale at Barney's, DeDe was out the door and on her way to a night and maybe a future with Nicky. I grabbed a quick bite and settled in with a pile of old magazines.

After I'd fallen asleep, I heard my girlfriend fumbling with the keys in an attempt to open the door. I got out of bed to let in a very drunk and disheveled DeDe, who was holding a paper bag of fast food and proceeded to horrify me with the evening's events.

Nicky had arrived almost two hours late in a chauffeur-driven stretch limousine while she waited for him at the bar drinking vodka Martinis on an empty stomach. His excuses included flat tires, red lights, and cops, all of which she bought, still impressed with the limo. She thought they would stay for a late dinner at the restaurant, but he said he preferred to eat elsewhere.

Elsewhere turned out to be the back seat of the limo with a bag of cold McDonald's hamburgers. She needed food badly, but turned to him instead, expecting to be kissed. He pushed her away. He told her she'd almost ruined several lives for her own selfish reasons and that he didn't want anything more to do with her.

"That bastard. Can you believe it?" she said, munching on a burger. "He drops me off here and throws this stuff out the window at me."

"Frankly, I can't picture him behaving that way."

"He called it retribution," she said.

"For what? Because you broke up with him? That's ancient history," I said, my mind going back to the recent dinner with Nicky.

"Well, mainly for what happened with Ben," she said.

"DeDe, it's late and you're drunk; but what the hell are you talking about?"

"Before I broke up with Nicky, I made up that story about how he seduced Ben's girlfriend and I got her to go along with it. Ben believed her and not Nicky, who swore it wasn't true, but it was too late. Ben moved out and broke up with his girlfriend. I guess she felt guilty later on and fessed up to Ben, who, of course, told Nicky. Too bad nobody let me in on the secret before I agreed to meet with him."

"Why on earth would you have done that? Why kill three relationships with a lie because you wanted to break up with Nicky?"

"Why? Because he disappointed me and I wanted everyone else to think he was a shit. Don't you get it? He promised something and didn't follow through. He fucking dropped out of Yale and I was supposed to stand by and wait for him to get his act together?" DeDe said. "After I married Mitch, I realized that I should have stood by Nicky because he's so successful now and that's why I came to New York when he called. Of course, I wanted to see you, but I need to change my life. Well, bestie, like you said, I guess it's ancient history. I'm pissed that he didn't even buy me dinner. He said he takes you to all the best places and I bet you don't have to do anything for it either."

"DeDe, you're drunk. You're my friend and I love you, but I don't want to hear any more. Go to bed."

"I'm sorry, Jessie, really, for everything I did. You know you're my bestest. I've got to lie down," she said, and a minute after throwing herself fully clothed on the bed, she vomited all over my Calvin Klein suit.

"Oh shit, I'm sorry," she said. "Let me go get cleaned up."

She came back out with my white terry cloth robe wrapped around her, but not belted. I folded back the blanket to make room for her.

"You know Laurel and I were lovers in high school," she said, settling back in bed. "Well, not real lovers, but we had lots of sex when I slept over and when we were in Europe. You never suspected, did you?"

I covered her and sat up.

"Then why on earth did you pretend to be so shocked last night? And, no, I didn't suspect anything back then, but I imagine you weren't above using her to get to Europe like you weren't above using me or Nicky to get what you wanted," I said. "I guess you missed the boat tonight with Nicky."

"I would have left Mitch for Nicky if he'd asked me to. Mitch is a decent guy; I'm just not the right wife for him. As for Europe? No way my parents could have afforded it, so Laurel told her folks she wouldn't go without me. They figured their daughter would be happier if she had a friend along. Laurel invited you as a courtesy. She knew you'd say no. So, bestie, disappointed in me?"

"Does it matter what I think? You know, you oughta sleep on the pull-out tonight. We'll talk tomorrow," I said, gently moving her off the bed.

"Oh please, I'm not a lesbian. I really wanted Nicky, but that's not happening. Now I'm going to have to find another way to stay in New York because I'm not staying married to Mitch. Shoulda listened to you on that one. I already told him I wanted a divorce before I left," she said, and stumbled out of the bedroom.

The evening had turned surreal and I found myself thinking about Miriam and the man she'd married. I'd been invited to the wedding, although not as member of the bridal party, and it was clear she'd chosen the right mate. I'd left behind a truly good person for a user. I hoped it wasn't too late to reunite with Miriam now that I'd learned a valuable lesson about friendship.

I found DeDe's note the next morning.

"Wow, bestest, I was so drunk last night and hope you forgive me for throwing up on your suit. Send me the cleaning bill. I think I told you I'm getting a divorce. I'll have to go back to Ohio to settle everything with Mitch. I already called Laurel and she said when I get back she and Eve will put me up until I find a job and place of my own. I think I overstayed my welcome with you. I still can't get over that she's with that old crow. Anyway, keep in touch. Love ya. DeDe."

DeDe didn't get in touch with me, nor did I try to reach her after she moved in with Laurel. Sometime after that, Eve called to see if I knew of any apartments available in my rent-controlled building. Although she and Laurel would remain business partners until one of them bought out the other, their personal relationship was over.

Nicky and I met for dinner and he went over his last evening with DeDe, and the shameful way he acted. On the bright side, he and Ben were able to resurrect their friendship and Ben ended up marrying his girlfriend. I told Nicky about Laurel and DeDe, which didn't surprise him, and then we decided to keep that part of our lives in the ancient history file.

We toasted the present and future with a couple of glasses of champagne, and I revealed my childhood crush on him. He smiled and said he enjoyed spending time with someone he trusts and feels comfortable with, someone who doesn't want anything from him except love. That someone turned out to be me.

THE TROUBLE WITH BOY TOYS

*B*oy Toy: "A significantly younger male in a sexual relationship," so says Wikipedia, the modern day Webster's. Not once, in the five years that I've known Jasper (who was twenty-five when we met and a little more than twenty years my junior) have I used that expression. Our older woman/younger man liaison wasn't a regular thing. With various girlfriends and boyfriends coming and going in between, and further complicated by his out-of-state move, we'd endured where other relationships had soured and gone south.

Jasper and I meet on a local dating site, BeachMates.com. After he pursues me with several intelligent sounding emails (with correct spelling and grammar yet), I decide to take him seriously enough to reply with more than a self-deprecating, "Pshaw, I'm old enough to be your mother. Sincerely yours, Rachael. " We agree to a coffee date.

I can still picture our first meeting at a well-known coffee house in Miami, haven to millions of internet hopefuls. Jasper removes his cap (a cap, mind you) as he stands to greet me. After we say hello, he tells me I'm kind of old to be so sexy. I take it as a compliment because I sense that's how he means it and counter by saying he's kind of young to be so charming. He orders me a double espresso, a high-caloric pseudo-java drink for himself, and with a convincing smile insists we split a wildly fattening almond croissant, which is the size of a Buick. We make small talk and although he doesn't care for my taste in music, he's thrilled that I own a small deep sea fishing business. There's snappy conversation and lots of laughs combined with a respectable amount of flirting, all of which lead to a second date for the following evening.

Jasper makes reservations at a restaurant featuring a lovely patio and after a candlelit dinner, he suggests a ride in his convertible (I try not to fret about my hair that I'd spent an hour blow-drying) to the beach where, hand in hand, we go for a long walk. He kisses me. I'm a goner, and not just because of the smooch. Candlelit dinners and romantic beach walks are mere promises in the land of on-line profiles. No one but Jasper has ever followed through.

I conquer the shyness of being in bed with a man half my age and begin to develop deep feelings for him. Jasper has the situation well under control. The most telling thing he'll say is, "I think about you more than I should," and occasionally utters the C word (chemistry). He loves my body, my hair, my big-screen television, our weekends on the boat, but never, even in the most passionate moments (okay, so they're all passionate), does he let slip the phrase, "I love you." I murmur it once and blame my indiscretion on the three Coronas I'd slugged down at the South Beach Tiki Bar. He admonishes me about blurting out dangerous words. I stumble around with explanations of why I said it and that it only refers to how precious he is, but the cat is out of the bag and the beast is now sitting right in the middle of the damned bedroom.

After his move halfway across the country, there's one terrifically intense weekend visit, which makes me wonder if I could truly be in love with him. If not, does that mean that there's something wrong with me? Being that physically close to someone has to produce some feelings of emotional intimacy, right? Do I want to love him? Do I want him to love me? What would happen then? Jasper and I occasionally venture out in public to grab a corn dog or some ice cream, but there is never any hand-holding or other displays of affection. Spectators, if they even care, may think he's my slightly younger brother (if only they would think that) or more likely my nephew, and lastly and most painfully, my son.

I have trouble accepting the fact that five years worth of fun and over-the-top lovemaking doesn't lead to a commitment, or at least a better connection. Jasper suffers two family tragedies, which he emails about, and I yearn to be of comfort to him, but he doesn't want it…or if he does, there is no expression of need. Except on my part. If I'd seen a raised eyebrow the one time I cautioned him to watch his cholesterol, do I really expect he's going to let me gather him to my virtual bosom for a soothing instant message session?

There are semi-lengthy stretches when we don't see each other or even communicate. Then, there's a late night phone call to say he can't stop thinking about me and how he'll never find anyone like me. Although I'd miss the sex like crazy, and the ego trip that empowered me to have ever attracted someone so young, hip, and cool, I do want him to find the right woman (okay, maybe a little like me) only twenty something years younger. Jasper and I both know that if someone age-appropriate and serious comes into either of our lives, we will be over. Neither of us wants to enter into a Prince Charles/Diana/Camilla triangle (He's too young to remember the Ari/Jackie/Maria Callas trilogy).

I moan and whine about the conundrum. My girlfriends tell me to shut it down because my heart will overtake my mind and that I should have stopped seeing Jasper a long time ago. They think my self-imposed agony will prevent me from meeting the right guy, even though men our age will have a tough time competing sexually with Jasper. But, they say while wagging their collective tongues and fingers at me, growing older with such a man will provide what is really important…the familiar.

I think about what I've given Jasper besides being a most appreciative lovemaking partner. He receives total acceptance without ulterior motives such as awaiting a marriage proposal or being forced into a clock-ticking baby conversation or reading ads for a nice house in the suburbs. He explained that technically I couldn't be classified as a cougar because he was the one who planned the seduction. I feel young and happy when he's around and it certainly doesn't hurt that he laughs at my jokes and thinks I'm hot, one of the more popular words of his generation.

Jasper invites me to visit him in his home town, but I explain that it might put him in an awkward position should we run into any of his friends or family. Like how would he introduce me? He says, innocently enough, as a friend. Even though I appreciate the gesture, I know better only because I'm older. Jasper is not my boy toy and I'm not his girlfriend. We're lovers with no possibility of a future.

Jasper is the man who brought me back to life at a disastrously low point in my existence. His first stop is at my house whenever he's in town, even before visiting his grandparents (yes, he has grandparents; both sets). I let him sleep over, but sneak him out before daybreak so my early bird neighbors won't get a whiff of what I imagine is a scandalous situation.

He speaks about his family in that tender manner the Gen-X, Y or Z population uses and is devoted to them as well as to his huge network of friends who call and text him night and day. He's carved out a successful career as a screenwriter and, thank God, is able to travel to Miami once a month for our heavenly trysts.

On Valentine's Day, Jasper arrives with two dozen of the reddest roses he must have paid a fortune for and a hand-written card using his favorite adjective to describe me—amazing. I tamely buy him a shirt, much as a loving aunt would do, damn it, and choose a silly card with two bears chatting about honey. My original thought was to replace the beaded necklace he'd always worn until it fell apart, so I schlep around the mall to find just the right thing, which I don't, and am so exhausted afterward that I almost call off our evening date, which I also don't. This isn't an O'Henry story, plus no one can stand that much irony.

I wonder how he would react if I decided to end our relationship. Jasper, who's probably never given any of this a nanosecond of thought, might wonder why I'm using the word relationship. "It is what it is," he says, but what, exactly, is it? You've heard people say they love someone, but they're not *in love* with them. I understand that; it's a concept I can sink my teeth into. I mean I love my cat, but I'm certainly not in love with her. So why can't I love Jasper without being in love with him?

I check my messages on BeachMates.com. The site doesn't disappoint. They match me up with John Robie and a man in my age bracket enters into the equation. He and I meet for dinner (I couldn't be unfaithful to Jasper and meet anyone else in a coffee shop) and for hours we never stop talking. He orders grilled fish, steamed broccoli, and salad with dressing on the side. I do the same because we're people in our fifties and that's how we eat, along with skim milk for our decafs; no juicy burgers with French fries like Jasper and I feed each other when no one's looking.

After two dates, John and I practically finish each other's sentences. He remembers Mello Rolls at the beach, and the double features we went to as kids in the sixties. We complain and trade war stories. He has high blood pressure; I have a bad knee. We're each divorced from long-term marriages, but it's okay because we've arrived at a stage in life when these things happen, and although it's not the mainstay of our conversation, it's allowable and acceptable (John has a son a year older than Jasper, but I can't go there yet).

The clear-cut remedy is to enter into a grown-up relationship with John, a wonderful man I could easily love and fall in love with. He's someone who, apart from being caring, funny, intelligent, and sexy, is familiar.

That would have been a Hollywood ending, only it wasn't mine. Three months into the new situation, I begin to miss Jasper so much that it erodes whatever's forming with John. I can't cut the cord, nor is Jasper willing to quietly step aside per our previous mutual agreement. Although Jasper had originally wished me good luck with John, his true desire was to be with me and I know that because he finally said it. (Turns out Jasper is well aware of the facts about Ari cheating on Jackie with Maria, and refuses to be a third party to any such unholy trinity).

Now, instead of sharing a life with John and the familiar, Jasper transfers to Miami and moves in with me. Together we discover the fun of not knowing so much about the same things. He

takes my hand on our beach strolls and every other place we frequent because I've stopped caring what people may think. Jasper
swears they're all jealous, of both of us. There's no mention of the
future. It is what it is.

LEAVING EASY

*W*hen we were children, my younger brother Dane had a stuffed toy dog he named Bruno Antony. Dane insisted that we call the dog by his full name at all times. Dane cherished Bruno Antony for years and they were rarely apart. Originally, the cute dog was soft and furry with long velvety ears, a reddish nose, and droopy lids. Hugs, kisses, and time had turned Bruno Antony into a beige rubbery creature with uneven eyes, jowls that hung down past his jaw, and the red nose lost forever.

One day, while having lunch with a client at Balthazar's busy Manhattan downtown bistro, I ran into an old friend of mine, Marnie Edgar. After barely recognizing her, I waved and gestured that I would stop by as soon as my meeting was over. The last time I'd seen Marnie she was a head-turner. Now, in 1985, a decade later, I was shocked to see that my friend's face had aged as poorly as Bruno Antony's toward the end of his years.

Marnie and I were thrown together during our first week at Syracuse University after our original roommates dropped out. It was a good fit because we were both majoring in economics and business management. Marnie was tall and slim with beautiful silky auburn hair and luminous blue eyes. We did well with our studies, but it was apparent that her ultimate goal was to pass Marrying a Wealthy Man 101.

During spring break of our junior year, while treating ourselves to a weekend in Newport, Rhode Island, Marnie met Roger Thornhill, a senior whose grandparents owned an enormous compound in the beautiful seaside city. Roger invited us for Sunday brunch and by the time we finished our Floating Islands, served by the silent staff standing by, Marnie had charmed his entire family. Two months later she became pregnant and convinced him to marry her, promising that she'd finish her education after the baby was born. His parents didn't consider it the best of situations, but concurred because they were enamored with Marnie, and more importantly, Roger was their only child and sole male heir to carry on the Thornhill name.

I was disgusted with Marnie for knowingly and deceitfully getting herself into this predicament in order to become part of a prosperous family and I refused to attend their wedding. I heard she carried a bouquet of lilies and wore a white satin sheath that stretched across her burgeoning stomach.

Roger went into business with his conservative father who ran a worldwide branding and logo firm. Mr. Thornhill believed Marnie would adapt to her corporate wife status as his own wife did years ago. Roger was wild for his bride because along with her natural beauty and charisma, she was exciting and adventurous, everything he wasn't. What Roger didn't know about was Marnie's excessive use of drugs, prescription and otherwise. Even back in our freshman year, Marnie ran with a fast crowd and there were many nights I had to put my stoned roommate to bed.

After Marnie and Roger returned from their honeymoon in Martinique, she called to ask if I'd like to spend a long weekend at their brownstone in the Back Bay section of Boston. Because I felt she was trying to set things right between us and because I felt guilty about missing her wedding, I accepted her invitation and we had an affectionate reunion, however incomplete.

I soon learned that Roger was seldom home, which left Marnie time to sip wine in the afternoon and smoke three or four joints in the evening. She ate and drank little else besides acrid coffee sitting on the burner, and reheated leftovers from a local take-out place.

I suffered her incoherent conversation for a day and a half before deciding to cut the weekend short. All the garbage she was inhaling and ingesting couldn't possibly have been good for the baby she was carrying. After a huge argument, which who knows if she even comprehended, I left and took the train back to school.

That was the last time I saw a still stunning Marnie until our chance meeting at the restaurant.

I'd heard, much to my relief, that Marnie had given birth to a healthy baby girl. Two years later she and Roger were blessed with another daughter. It was shortly after the birth of their second child that I received a call from Roger. Marnie was out of control, a circumstance that made him uneasy about leaving her alone with their two young children. He tried to convince her to attend addiction support meetings, but like most people who are in denial she refused to go. Roger continued to discuss their personal life, something I didn't feel comfortable with. He hadn't known what he was getting himself into before they married, and now was in too deep to extricate himself from an intolerable situation.

His parents had grown disgusted with Marnie's unbecoming behavior at family and company social events, but remained solidly against divorce. Mr. Thornhill told Roger to get control of his wife even if he had to ship her off to a rehab facility.

I explained to Roger that while thoughts of my former friend had entered my mind throughout the years, I never had the stomach to contact her. Marnie's attitude the last time we were together had been unbearable and getting involved at this point held no appeal for me. There was nothing I could do to help either one of them, so I suggested he consult a psychiatrist and wished him good luck before hanging up. I'd been Marnie's caregiver long ago; now it was up to her husband, however frustrated he found himself.

After ending the meeting with my client at Balthazar's, I walked over to Marnie's table and asked if she cared for some company. Her eyebrows arched in a "why not" expression and she offered me a seat.

"Lucy, it's wonderful to see you. How about a drink or a glass of wine?" she said.

I ordered a pot of tea, more as a prop to fiddle with than anything else, while we talked. Marnie was sipping a champagne cocktail prompting me to regret having acknowledged her. With slurred words she went on to recount her side of the story.

She had stopped taking drugs for a short while after the birth of her second daughter and was determined to become a fit mother and the wife Roger thought he had married. Certain she could still bewitch him, Marnie was confident there was no danger of his leaving, but despite the help of a competent housekeeper, the daily care of her two children had become too heavy a task for her. She began using amphetamines to ignore the monotony of her days and Valium at night to get a few hours rest. Wine and marijuana were ever present to help maintain a buzz that enabled her to sleepwalk through dirty diapers and meals.

One day she'd left the baby screaming in her highchair for two hours after passing out during a lunchtime feeding. She was awakened by a surprise visit from her mother-in-law, who stirred Marnie into consciousness before calling her son.

That night, after his distraught mother left to go home, Roger explained to Marnie that if she didn't agree to stop drinking and drugging herself to death he would resort to having her committed. Her charms had worn thin; he was swamped and pressured at the office with little time to worry about her or his children's daily welfare. Roger told her he didn't care what his family or business partners thought; he would divorce her if she couldn't pull herself together.

Roger hired a nanny the next day to care for the children and told Marnie to work on herself.

"Ah, Lucy, what my husband didn't realize was that with the children and house being looked after, my self-destruction had only been facilitated. It was a celebration for me the day the nanny started. I'd drink wine or vodka, fiddle with a little coke, pop a few pills, and hang out in my robe; maybe nap or watch cartoons with the kids," she said, before finishing her cocktail. "At least that's what I thought I was doing," she continued, with a wry laugh. "Seems like I was wandering through the house screaming and crying. I begged the nanny not to call Roger, but what choice did she have?"

"Weren't your girls frightened seeing you like that," I said, horrified at her account.

"You'd think, but I guess they were used to me at that point. The girls were in pre-school and kindergarten for part of the day, but yes, there were times when the little one ran to her room when I had one of my sessions," she said, signaling the waiter for another drink.

"I don't know how the nanny stayed as long as she did, but in the end she left even though Roger offered to double her salary. Roger kept hiring more nannies and they kept quitting after a few months, no matter what he paid them. His parents made us sell the Boston place and demanded that we move into their compound so that his mother could be on hand to keep an eye on me. You'd think all those rich old broads up there drinking their Pink Ladies at the club would have a little compassion. My mother-in-law moved us into one of the large guesthouses with my husband's blessings and he was only too happy to commute to Boston, stay in a hotel, and get away from me. What could I do? I had no money of my own."

"You could have gone back to college after the kids were a little older. Surely Roger would have encouraged that. Wasn't that your original plan when you got married?" I said, trying to soften my business-like demeanor.

"We discussed it, but I wasn't sober long enough to fill out an application," she said, taking a long pause before continuing. "I don't blame him for the divorce. By the time I realized he was seeing one of the Newport blue bloods it was too late to pull myself together. Look at my hair. My eyes. Am I someone who could make a husband fall back in love with her? Hardly," she said, this time with a pitiful laugh.

"But you could have gone to rehab. It wasn't hopeless," I said.

"Lucy, the eternal optimist. Don't you think I tried that? Two or three of them. I'd stay clean for a few weeks and then fall back.

I managed to kick the drugs, not the booze.

Roger left me and married the woman he was seeing, Lisa Fremont—how's that for a fancy name? He easily retained custody of our daughters and as much as I loved them, I knew it was for the best. Roger arranged for supervised visits every other weekend if I agreed to go back to rehab, which I did. He said he had little hope for me. I guess he wasn't the only one," she said, giving me a distressed, but knowing, look.

"Marnie, I'm sorry. I should have been there for you," I said, the words sounding false even to me. In order to pick up the conversation, I asked why she was in New York.

"My husband was generous with alimony, which allows me to get away from Newport—yes, I still live on their compound—and come to New York a few times a year. I stay at a fancy hotel, drink champagne and hope to run into an old friend. Just kidding about that last part, because I never expected to meet you today. You look so put together and judging from your outfit and handbag, I'd say you've done well for yourself. I like to pretend that I'm that person too…desirable."

"I'm glad we ran into each other. I had no idea of what you were going through," I said, trying to shake off a chill.

"Now you know everything. Still upset with me?" Marnie said. "You sure as hell were when I got pregnant. You wouldn't even return my calls after that weekend in Boston. You must have known how badly I needed a friend, but I guess it was easier to dump me than to reason with me."

Taking a sip of tea before answering, I said, "Marnie, do you really think I could have done any good? That's your fourth glass of champagne in an hour and you'll probably continue once I leave. I'm not your therapist. I was your friend, but if you think I'm hanging around to wipe up your mess like I did in college, you've got the wrong person. I have nothing left to give."

After plunking down ten dollars I said good bye and stood up from the table, ready to make my exit.

"Is that what you do, Lucy?" Marnie said. "Leave? You wouldn't even come to my wedding. Don't you know what that did to me? Walking down the aisle in Roger's church without you as my maid of honor? I had to tell my mother that you had the flu. I couldn't tell my in-laws the truth either. Funny thing is how they accepted me at first, but I botched that up early on.

I know how serious my problems were, and maybe still are, but why are you always so damned judgmental? Yes, I know you took care of me in college; how many times did you remind me about that? Yes, the weekend in Boston was awful for you, but we'd been so close before that happened. It was torture when you walked away. I don't blame you for anything; I admit it's my fault. I have an addictive personality, but does that stop you from being a friend? That's what I'm asking you now. Please be my friend again. Make me laugh like you used to. Don't leave."

Shoving the champagne to the side, Marnie dabbed her eyes with a white napkin. I sat down. She was right. I was a *leaver*. As soon as anything went the slightest bit awry I gave it up. I'd left men who pursued me because I didn't care for their choice of careers, my synagogue because one of the sermons didn't appeal to me, and anyone or place that didn't suit my exact needs or expectations. I'd ended friendships over insignificant quarrels, dropped clients who didn't call back on time and worst of all, deserted Marnie when she needed me the most. What was it in my makeup that caused me to give up so easily?

"I'm willing to try to quit drinking—I tossed all the pills after my last rehab stint—if you promise to give up your damned lecturing and moralizing," she said, "and maybe get your sense of humor back. That disappeared around the same time I got pregnant."

"I'm so sorry, Marnie. I can't believe I treated you so shabbily. I need help also," I said, using the other napkin to dry my eyes although I was smiling at her last remark. "Maybe there's a group out there that takes in alcoholics and cold-hearted women who throw their friends away."

"If there isn't, we'll start one. Why don't you stay in the hotel with me tonight, please Lucy. There are two beds in my suite, let's start over. I promise I'll go to AA when I get home. I can't be the only alcoholic up there. My mother-in-law's been pretty decent to me, mainly because of the kids; I'm sure she'd be happy to find a therapist."

"Maybe she can find one for me too," I said, only half joking.

"Right now, we need each other as friends. Maybe tomorrow, if you're not working, we could go to one of those fancy makeup counters and you can help me get this ragged face back together."

I didn't know what she meant because when I looked at her face, as precious to me as a fine painting, it was no longer something that could be compared to an old stuffed animal with the ridiculous name of Bruno Antony. I smiled and touched her cheek.

"Tomorrow's Saturday. I'm free all day. In the meanwhile, I only had a salad before with that skinny bitch client of mine and I'm starving. Let's order something to eat."

LOUIS BERNARD

*T*he night I saved Louis Bernard's life was the night I should have let him die like the flea on a dog he was. My husband Jonathan and I were acknowledging seven hot and cold years of marriage at the trendy Greek restaurant, Old Stove Pub, in Wainscott, New York when we heard a stifled, choking sound. It was coming from a man who had both hands at his throat, the universal sign that he was, indeed, choking. I jumped up and executed your basic Heimlich maneuver, which expelled a chunk of steak. The piece of meat landed smack in the middle of a plate in front of fellow diner, Ralph Lauren, who swore he had just finished his *moussaka*. After the entire group in the small restaurant applauded me, I was introduced to the man whose life I'd just saved, Louis Bernard, as well as to his dinner companions. I said I was glad to have helped and went back to join Jonathan who, by the way, hadn't even bothered to look up.

"Finished with your celebrity search, Maddy?" he said.

This had been one of our cold years.

I met Jonathan Elster in 2004 at the top floor gym of my Aunt Marion's luxury apartment building in Manhattan. He was a guest of his boss who owned a large advertising agency and the penthouse apartment. After a series of my bad boyfriends and Jonathan's broken engagement, he and I began to date and walked down the aisle a year later.

I'd been a terrible college student and my parents stopped paying for my education during my sophomore year at Hofstra University on Long Island. They nudged me out of the house unless I started to work and pay rent. Aunt Marion had a kinder heart and took me in, rent-free, provided I found a job within a reasonable amount of time and paid back some of the money my parents had wasted on me.

My grade point average had been about a one, but I was pretty good with making up catchy slogans and a poem here and there, so I began an online business for people who wanted specialized greeting cards, invitations, and the like. I was shocked by the amount of orders that came through my website and in a few months I was able to begin paying off the loan to my folks. They would have welcomed me back home to live, but I much preferred living in my new digs on Park Avenue with my aunt.

Aunt Marion still refused to take a dime from me. Her late husband, Ambrose Chapel, died unexpectedly in his forties at the height of his career as a day trader and left my aunt well off. They'd had no children and she refused to be fixed up with available gentlemen her age, several of whom lived in the building, so I was as close to a daughter as she'd ever have. It was a great arrangement because not only did I have my own bedroom, but I also had the spare room, which having been originally planned for a maid, was now my work space.

Jonathan and I were married in a small ceremony and he moved into my aunt's apartment, which was easily three times the size of his place in the Kips Bay area. He worked long hours and offered to help out with expenses, which Aunt Marion didn't need, but graciously accepted.

My husband's true passion was sculpting in clay. I'd known about it, but had never been to his studio, which he shared with two other would-be artists down in Soho. Jonathan's job at the agency was all-consuming and when it became so stressful that he broke out in hives all over his body, Aunt Marion and I persuaded him to quit and devote himself full-time to his artful endeavors. I had enough money coming in from my business and it wouldn't be long before Jonathan started to sell his work.

My husband was easy going and handy around the house and my aunt enjoyed having him live with us. Jonathan seemed so knowledgeable about his craft and we felt sure that being right in the middle of the art world would help lead to his success. After much prodding, he invited Aunt Marion and me to visit his studio. He'd previously kept us at bay saying that he hadn't completed anything worth seeing yet and that the other artists preferred not to be disturbed.

One Sunday, the three of us went out for breakfast at a local coffee shop and then headed downtown to the studio. His fellow artists, who worked in oil, had taken a substantial amount of their paintings to pitch at a few galleries and weren't due back until after five. Aunt Marion and I were so excited to finally see the results of my husband's efforts that we hardly noticed the five flights of stairs we had to climb to reach his work space.

"Jonathan, we're going to have to find you your own studio with an elevator, or at least one that's on the ground floor," said my generous aunt, who was now out of breath.

"That's very kind of you, Marion, but this is fine for now. Let me unlock the door and get you some water. We have a small fridge," he said.

If there's a slogan out there to describe the utter horribleness of what we saw, I'm unaware of it. Piece after piece of clay globs, twenty-six in all, and not one had any charm or artistic value, at least to the layman's eye. They were hideous and I was speechless. Aunt Marion was not only speechless and out of breath, but had also collapsed on the studio floor, apparently fainting from shock at the disappointing collection. As I splashed a little cool water on her wrists I realized her eyes were open and lifeless. Jonathan had already called 911 and was performing CPR, but Aunt Marion was dead long before the paramedics made it up the five flights.

After the funeral and reading of the will, which left almost everything to me with a decent sized portion to my parents, I suggested we move out of Manhattan to East Hampton. In the months that followed Aunt Marion's death, we suffered her personal loss and our marriage suffered as well. Jonathan felt useless because he wasn't bringing in a salary and furthermore was envious that I was the beneficiary of a couple of million dollars and the apartment and still had my business, which I continued to run because I enjoyed it. I needed to separate myself from my brooding, restless husband who spent less and less time at his studio and more hours at home watching television and playing loud video games.

Our marriage, which had turned antagonistic, could possibly have a better chance of succeeding without the pressures of the city. Coupled with the fact that Jonathan hadn't sold even one sculpture, well, you didn't have to be Sigmund Freud to figure out where his hostility was coming from. Jonathan, although still on the warpath, was in favor of the move and in the fall of 2008, at the worst possible financial time, we sold the apartment to Jonathan's former boss. He gifted it to his son who'd come into the successful advertising agency, the same business that had gifted my husband with hives.

We moved out to the east end of Long Island, and purchased a nice-sized home halfway between the beach and the village of East Hampton. There was plenty of room for Jonathan to turn the apartment over the garage into a studio, which I convinced him would be a splendid idea. He set up shop and kept busy, but our relationship didn't improve.

We went on like that for several more years with a disintegrating marriage, my business waning due to a poor economy and, worst of all, Jonathan was still unable to sell a single piece of sculpture to any of the galleries scattered throughout the Hamptons or on the celebrated north fork of Long Island. We kept up appearances by going out to dinner with friends and routinely celebrated our birthdays and anniversaries, which led us to the Old Stove Pub on that fated night when I saved Louis Bernard's life.

After Jonathan's rude remark to me that evening, we were about to go one-on-one over his attitude when Louis stopped by our table. He introduced himself to Jonathan and insisted we be his guests for lunch the next day at the prestigious Atlantic Golf Club. My mouth dropped open, but I closed it in time to shoot my husband a "don't you dare say no" look. I had become a compulsive, but erratic, golfer and was known as Tiger Gump at our own low-key club, the South Fork. After accepting his invitation, Louis thanked me again and we said good night.

Louis was seated at a large booth when the maître d' ushered us into the Atlantic dining room. The captain suggested the lobster salad, which we agreed sounded wonderful, and Louis asked to see the wine list. The conversation centered on golf until Jonathan mentioned that he had given up the sport in order to devote his spare time to sculpting.

"Now that's a coincidence," Louis said. "I'm about to convert a store in town—you know, that old Goth place—to an art gallery. It's all very hush-hush right now, so please don't say anything."

We promised not to divulge his secret and because we were all getting along so well, Louis invited me to join him for a round of golf on Friday at the Atlantic. I accepted with pleasure, happy there would be enough time for me to buy a new outfit in town.

Jonathan had begun to sulk when the conversation turned back to golf until Louis cemented their relationship by saying, "I'd love to see your work. You never know…I may be able to take some of it on consignment for my opening. How about if I stop by one evening?" Jonathan perked right up and accepted his offer and issued one of his own.

"Why not have dinner with us this Saturday night? Maddy's a terrific cook," said the husband I hardly recognized anymore.

"That sounds fine as long as I won't be needing any first aid!" Louis said. We had a brief laugh, thanked our host, and said good bye.

I splurged (to be frank, we had to watch our expenses since the apartment sold at a low point and the new house was way more than we should have spent) and bought myself a pair of Burberry Capri pants with a matching knit shirt, and a straw hat trimmed with red grosgrain ribbon for my golf date at the Atlantic.

Louis had suggested he and I meet for breakfast in the club's dining room before joining up with another twosome, but as I was about to valet my car on Friday morning, I saw Louis heading my way with a picnic basket in hand.

"Maddy, how about having breakfast with me on the beach? We have enough time—we can't tee off 'til ten o'clock anyway—what d'you say?"

I didn't have to think twice about the most romantic offer I'd had in years.

"Do you mind if we take your car?" Louis said, as he hopped into the passenger seat. "The Benz is in the shop, and my old station wagon is filled with supplies."

I put the top down on my Saab, and ten minutes later we were on the beach. We didn't have a blanket, and breakfast turned out to be a couple of stale donuts and lukewarm coffee, but the sun was bright and the ocean calm, so we sat and dunked and talked until I realized it was way past our tee time.

"Oh forget it," Louis said. "We'll play another day. I can always get us in."

I dropped Louis back at the club and drove home in my sandy Burberry's. When I arrived, I saw that my husband had been busy. Every piece of distorted, misshapen sculpture, including the ones that couldn't sell at the East Hampton Clothesline Art Sale, where everyone sells something, were now displayed in our living room. He was preparing for Saturday night, setting up a private viewing for Louis. He gave me an abbreviated tour and I wisely complimented each piece using words like profound, passionate, intimate, and anything else I could drum up for his hum-drum work.

Saturday came and Jonathan insisted on being in charge of grocery shopping. I had planned to put together a simple dinner of poached salmon with fresh corn and a salad, but wanting to make the right impression, my husband was adamant that we serve filet mignon, so off he went to the local butcher shop to buy steaks that cost almost as much as my Burberry's. After that, he stopped at Citarella's, a gourmet shop well known for its fancy cheeses, appetizers, and desserts, and dropped at least another hundred, although he refused to show me the bill. Jonathan wasn't normally this extravagant, and even though he was overdoing it, this was not the time to nit-pick.

Louis arrived early, cursing himself because he'd left a bottle of chilled Cristal champagne back at his house. There was hardly a place to sit for a drink in our art-laden living room, so we decided to look through the sculpture before dinner. Louis was full of praise and at the end of the tour, offered to take all of

Jonathan's work on consignment for his new gallery. Jonathan's face lit up like an operating room and agreed.

It was sometime later that evening, I think while sipping our dessert wine, a St. Supery Moscato, which was a flawless match with Citarella's crème brulee, that Louis let his cool slip. He told us about the problems he was having opening the gallery. A great part of his bankroll had gone into purchasing exquisite paintings in Europe and now the present shop owners were demanding an additional fifty thousand dollars in key money that he couldn't get his hands on. The dilemma was getting worse by the minute because the European goods were due to arrive any day, and there would be no storage space for them.

"I feel guilty because Jonathan's work is so salable and compatible with the paintings that are coming in," Louis said. "I'm afraid I'd be doing you a disservice by taking them off the market until the gallery is ready and I'm not sure when that will be."

Louis appeared to be embarrassed about being cash poor, but Jonathan was already seeing his name up in lights at the Louvre on Main Street. He jumped right in with an offer without so much as a "let's discuss it first" glance from me.

"We can lend you the money; we can be part owners."

It was such a pleasure to see Jonathan so elated about the project, or anything, that I let it go. It wouldn't break us, and if the loan brought our marriage back to where it had been before Aunt Marion passed away, it'd be worth the fifty thousand. Someone whose life you've just saved certainly isn't going to screw you. I wrote out the check and an informal partnership agreement and Louis promised to call us with all the details within a couple of days. He and Jonathan loaded up Louis's station wagon—the Benz was still in the shop—with the clay pieces that maybe I had misjudged, and we waved goodbye.

Louis was fantastic company, notwithstanding his financial difficulties, and Jonathan and I had both been seduced by his good looks, charm, and suavity. Since we couldn't have him, we had each other in one of the most stimulating romps of our marriage. In the afterglow, my husband talked about our new art gallery.

Our partner called a few days later and asked us to meet him for lunch at Rowdy Hall, a local pub, to hear some important news. All three of us decided on the house favorite of fish and chips and after a few glasses of ale, Louis let us in on the latest details. The loan had been satisfactory for the sellers, but now the shipping company was billing him eight thousand dollars for storage. Because Louis had paid a million and a half dollars for the paintings, this extra charge didn't seem like an outrageous sum to him, but he still didn't have the available cash. I nervously wrote out another check after which he brightened considerably until I mentioned playing golf at the Atlantic.

"Sorry Maddy, my sciatica's acting up from moving all of Jonathan's work. There'll be plenty of time for golf after the opening," he assured me. When the lunch check came, Louis made a weak attempt to reach for his wallet, but Jonathan put him off saying it was our treat.

"Thanks guys, I'll be back in touch very soon," he said, leaving the restaurant.

On our way out of Rowdy Hall we ran into Lars Thorwald. Lars was famous for his weekly columns in the local newspaper and we'd gotten to know him while drinking Margaritas together at the Blue Parrot Café, a popular hangout for year 'rounders. Lars knew more about what went on in the Hamptons than anyone else and had written several successful novels based on the local lifestyle.

"Hi Maddy, Jon," he said. "Do you have a minute? I saw that you were having lunch with Louis Bernard. I know all about how you saved his life, which was damned heroic, but I was wondering what else you know about him."

"Well, I know he loves to play golf," I said. "He's a member over at the Atlantic and..." I stopped short of mentioning the secretive art gallery.

"Maddy," Lars said, "Louis is not a member of the Atlantic Golf Club. He went to school with their golf pro and once a month they comp him for a round of golf and lunch in the dining room. I heard they recently rescinded those privileges because he went crazy last week ordering lobster salad and a ninety-dollar bottle of wine. Apparently, he was trying to impress a couple of new chumps…oh, Maddy, I'm sorry, that was probably you and Jonathan.

Anyway, he's not a bad sort, very charismatic and lots of fun to have around; we all take him out to dinner now and then. Just don't give him any money you can't afford to lose. That's happened more than once out here and at one point, rumor had it that he'd amassed a pretty big bankroll. No one knew how he got it, or if they did, they weren't talking. Please be careful about getting into any of his deals," Lars said.

Jonathan and I were silent. We'd been taken. We croaked out a feeble thank you and stumbled out of the restaurant.

Louis didn't return our calls or texts for the next month, so we decided to formulate our own plan. I enticed him to meet us for dinner at the Palm, which no one in their right mind would turn down, least of all a man who didn't have spare change. He met us at the restaurant, and I was alarmed at his appearance. He had two-day-old stubble, he needed a haircut, and his sports jacket was frayed around the collar. Louis must have sensed my uneasiness because he mentioned that he'd been working at the gallery to the exclusion of everything else and was sorry he'd neglected to call us. After his second Bloody Mary and a twenty-dollar crabmeat cocktail, Louis was almost giddy as he began to recount how well the plans were going.

"Louis," Jonathan said, interrupting him, "Maddy and I were wondering when we could take a look at the space. You haven't returned any of our messages and whenever we pass by, the windows are covered up and no one comes to the door. We're supposed to be partners."

"Of course we are, but I assumed you'd prefer to be the silent type and not get involved with the nitty-gritty of it all. As for the gallery, I wouldn't want you to see it for weeks yet, maybe even a couple of months," Louis said. "No one's allowed in; I'm doing all the work myself. Now that you mention it, supplies cost more than I expected, so I'll have to borrow a few thousand more…maybe ten or fifteen…if that's okay with you."

Jonathan lowered the boom. "Louis, we want out. We don't think that this project is ever going to get off the ground and we've been advised to dissolve the partnership. We're willing to write off the fifty-eight thousand dollars we gave you if you'll sign this note saying that all future debts and liabilities will be incurred by you alone. We'll each get a copy." We'd written this *tour de force* by ourselves, being too embarrassed to admit our naiveté to our financial advisor who'd repeatedly warned us about overspending.

Louis paused long enough to order a double-cut veal chop, hash browns, and creamed spinach before saying, "I'm sorry you feel that way, but if you don't have confidence in me, then I can't blame you for backing out. Even though we agreed to split everything fifty/fifty, costs and profits, I don't want to lose your friendship. That's more important than business. I'll sign the note, but I think you're making a mistake."

"We'll take our chances," Jonathan said, with a gracious but satisfied smile. Louis signed the note and we finished dinner making small talk because East Hampton's a small town and we didn't want to make enemies either. As Louis was leaving, with a slice of cheesecake wrapped to go, he asked about Jonathan's sculptures.

"They're all yours," Jonathan said.

"Are you sure? That's quite a bit of work to give away."

"Absolutely."

"Would you mind if I add a note to our agreement so we're all nice and legal on that? We can both initial it," he said.

Jonathan and Louis each took a copy of the signed dissolution contract, with the rider, and he left while my husband and I had a celebratory cognac.

"I'm going to donate all my sculpting supplies to the high school. I don't need to be reminded of what a fool I was," Jonathan said.

That was the last we saw of Louis Bernard. For six months. Then one day as I was walking along Main Street, I noticed that the Gothic store previously called The Gauntlet was no longer boarded up, but in its place was an art gallery. Antique pine planks had replaced the black painted floors, and the blood red walls were now plastered white. I didn't have to look up to know that the royal blue sign said "Louis Bernard." I peered inside the locked gallery to see the new owner standing behind a granite-topped desk going through some leaflets. He looked up, smiled, and strolled over to unlock the door.

"Maddy, how wonderful to see you. You look beautiful. How do you like the gallery? It's a shame you and Jonathan didn't stay in our partnership."

Louis was aglow in the natural lighting of the gallery and his eyes were brighter than any of the magnificent paintings that hung on two of the walls. I was flabbergasted when I saw what adorned the remainder of the space: Jonathan's pieces, each on a Lucite pedestal.

"Those are ours!" I said.

"Not anymore," Louis reminded me. "Jonathan specifically instructed me to keep all his work. I believe we each signed a contract to that effect."

"But, Louis," I said, sounding whinier than I wanted to, "when people find out that these are Jonathan's and that you duped us out of all that money, no one will set foot in here."

"Maddy," he said with a tsk, "are you really going to tell people that tale? I didn't swindle you out of anything; it was your decision. No one will know whose they are, nor will they care. You're certainly not going to show our contract around town. Let's leave the sculptor's name as unknown. People love that. Do you mind?"

He was right on all counts. We'd been scared off by the illusion of his deceiving us; there'd be no sense in trying to prove anything because we'd signed, sealed, and delivered everything over to Louis.

"Well, Maddy," Louis said, "no hard feelings, I hope. Why don't you and Jonathan stop by tomorrow night for the grand opening? Everyone will be here."

When I got home, I could see my husband waiting on the front porch for me wildly gesticulating with a piece of paper.

"Maddy, you'll never guess! I have a client, Ralph Lauren. His assistant sent over this agreement today saying Ralph had heard about me from my ex-boss's son, you know, the one who bought Marion's apartment, and now Ralph wants me to work exclusively for his companies in the advertising department. I can turn my studio into an office and work from home. Can you believe it? You know, I've always felt bad about the money I suggested we give to Louis. I'm sure I'll earn it back in half a year." Jonathan held me in a bear hug until he noticed I was crying.

"Maddy, what is it?" he said. I filled him in on Louis's gallery, but nothing could burst his bubble. "Let's go to his party tomorrow night. I don't care about that old crap of mine; he'll never sell any of it. I can't even believe he's going to show it. Sweetheart, I'm going back to what I'm good at."

When we arrived at Louis's gallery opening, it was jammed with the most beautiful people you usually only read about. Jonathan spotted Mr. Lauren and hurried over to introduce himself. I bumped into Lars who said in amazement, "Well, I certainly wish I'd lent Louis money this time. He's going to make a fortune here and look how clever he is exhibiting sculpture by an unknown artist. Personally, I think the stuff is dreadful, but leave it to Louis to make it a hit."

People were not only looking that night, they were buying, and quicker than you could say Heimlich maneuver, eight red sold stickers went up on all those damned Lucite stands holding Jonathan's work.

A few months later, my husband and I were celebrating our anniversary at East Hampton's Nick and Toni's Restaurant when we heard a loud sputtering coming from the next table. We looked at each other, put down our drinks and yelled, "Check, please!"

SUBURBAN VAMPIRE

*Y*ou try to lead a normal life, well as normal as possible, but as a Jewish vampire (kosher yet) I was having difficulties. Three hours after I moved into my new home on Mockingbird Lane—yes, I know it's where the Munsters lived, but that was total fiction—they were total hicks. Anyway, back to my afternoon. A neighbor arrived late in the day with a soggy brown cake. Mind you, it was winter and the sun had just set, so it was safe to open the door to suburban homemaker, Joanna Eberhart, who announced she lived right next door. Lucky me.

"Hi neighbor! Walter and I saw the moving truck here all day, but we didn't see hide nor hair of you. Soooo," she said, stringing out the word after using a double negative, "here's a little welcome present. I baked it myself," Joanna said, proud of her misshapen slab of sugar, butter and flour. "The Hospitality Wagon should be coming around tomorrow. I'm on the committee, and told them to be here at two, is that okay?"

Was she freakin' kidding me? In the middle of the day? That definitely wouldn't work.

"And you're going to have to give them your last name for our records; it only says Plage on the mailbox. Gee, I hope I'm pronouncing that right," Joanna said.

"Just perfect. It means beach; my parents were French," I said, repeating the idiotic instructions from the Count.

The Count, a notorious social climber who knows from nothing, only gave me a first name, adding that a French moniker would sound "more classier"—his grammar, not mine.

"You'll tell people your parents were French," he said. I'm pretty feisty for a female vampire, but you cannot cross the Count. It's just not done. "I need you to infiltrate suburbia to find out if it's suitable for our kind. It's part of our cross-culture mission," he said. Since the Count doesn't know his ass from anyone's elbow, least of all his own, I let it pass and took the job.

So now I'm standing here with Betty Crocker and since I wasn't real fast with human repartee I came up with the first thing that popped into my mind.

"It's Vein. Veinstein, I mean. I'm Jewish. And thanks for the cake, but I can't eat it. I'm a vegan and keep kosher," I said, blurting out a lie along with the truth.

"Oh? But there's no meat in the cake and it's vegetable oil, not butter," Joanna said with that "love my cake, love me" look in her eyes.

"My mistake. I meant I'm allergic to White Zinfandel and gluten, so there's no way I can eat the cake. I love meat," I said, wangling my way out of the conversation.

"But I use almond flour; it's gluten-free, and you must come over for a barbeque tonight. It's been such a warm winter and we want to take advantage of it. I won't take no for an answer. Walter, that's my ever-loving hubby, wanted to meet you, but he's watching football or some other manly sport. See you later. Seven o'clock and don't bother bringing anything; we have a box of prime steaks that my sister-in-law sent us for Christmas. How do you like yours?" she said, moving her head from side to side trying to keep the conversation going, so she could sneak a peek into my living room.

"Rare. Very rare. See you then," I said. "I have a ton of things to do."

Like planning her demise…and not for the obvious reasons. Joanna was blonde, rail-thin, pale, and short, and definitely not worth the blood-letting; I just didn't want her snooping around.

Since I had nothing in the house to snack on and the only Jewish deli in town closed early on Friday nights, I made some coffee and had a sliver of Joanna's cake, which she insisted I take. Wow! It was fabulous. I'd never tasted anything like it in my several hundred years of being undead. I wonder what she put in it; I'd have to ask tonight at the barbeque. While I was changing out of my black tights and tee into a swingy black jersey dress, I felt pretty good. Calm. Covering up my identity wouldn't be that difficult and I might even let Joanna live. I'd be affable this evening and blend in with the neighbors.

When I arrived at eight, the party was in full swing and the smell of beef cooking over an open flame was tantalizing, yet nauseating at the same time. I'm certain it wasn't kosher meat, but I did make exceptions outside the house.

"Well, you must be our new neighbor, Plage," said the chef, who introduced himself as Walter. "Go get yourself a drink and I'll have the steaks ready in a jiffy. They're not kosher," he confessed, confirming my suspicions, "but I bet you can cheat once in a while. Rare, right?"

"Thanks, Walter. Actually, make mine well done if it's not too much trouble," I said, surprising myself. Being affable was one thing, but asking for meat that wasn't dripping with blood? Why would I put in such a request? Before I had a chance to mull it over further, Joanna grabbed hold of me and introduced me to her crowd. I almost felt guilty looking for a nice thick neck because these people were so welcoming and friendly. Even though I was due for a transfusion I decided to wait it out until I was sure of the donor.

After dinner we sat around in Joanna's Colonial/Post-Modern living room with one of those sofas where six or seven people could recline at the same time, and our hostess sliced up another cake, identical to the one she'd brought over to me. I couldn't resist. I had to find out what was in that confection.

"Joanna, I've never tasted such a delicious cake. I simply can't identify the exact flavor. Do you mind revealing your secret?" I said, with just a hint of a smile, not wanting to bare my incisors.

"Everyone loves Joanna's cakes," said a plump woman named Charmaine, a prospective gourmet meal ticket for me, although the thought of blood was now making me queasy.

"Oh, you all make such a fuss over my cake, but it's really simple...I chop up dried figs and add them to the batter," said my hostess. "Plage, are you okay? You look all flushed?"

Flushed? A vampire? That's a shade we don't turn. And I was far from okay. I almost passed out on the spot. FIGS—the one food that is Kryptonite to all vampires. It kills our abilities and powers, including being able to turn into a bat, which has been mighty helpful throughout the centuries; but on the other hand, it could be nice not to have to sleep in a coffin. It was too late to overturn the events of the evening because even one small bite of a fig was enough to begin humanizing a vampire. I'd felt strange after my afternoon nibble, but now it was coming on in full force. After a short coughing fit, I addressed the group sitting or reclining in the room with me.

"I'm fine, Joanna. Just remembered I was supposed to be at services tonight; I'll be sure to go in the morning," I said, hiding the true nature of my discovery.

"Plage," said Bobbi Markowe, my backdoor neighbor. "Why don't I pick you up and we'll go together."

"Thanks Bobbi, that sounds lovely. If you wouldn't mind, do you think we could stop at Macy's afterward, I need some new sheets," I said, and took another bite of cake.

His

THE DATING GAME

*S*ince my blind date Winnie Verloc had just ordered her second pricy Mojito, I knew I had to stick to club soda if I was going to be able to pay for dinner.

My friend, Scotty Ferguson, had suggested that Winnie might be exactly the type of lady I'd be attracted to. Winnie was his travel agent and according to Scotty's description, she was blond, tall, and shapely. I had to admit she sounded perfect, but I'd said that before. Since my divorce three years ago, for some reason I can't seem to find the right woman. Ordinarily, I'm the easiest guy in the world to get along with.

We met at the bar in an upscale restaurant that Winnie had suggested, a place that would stretch my budget, but to which I had agreed nonetheless in order to make a good impression. A few minutes into our conversation I realized that Winnie had an obsessive, or was it compulsive, type of personality—repeating the same remarks two and three times verbatim. She was a bore and I was already into the bar tab for thirty bucks. As she was about to order a third Mojito, I suggested we sit down for dinner. The captain led the way to a decent enough table and, of course, asked if he could bring us another round. Winnie said yes.

"I love the lamb here," she cooed, as soon as we were seated. "Want to share a rack?"

"Sure, why not," I said, almost getting apoplexy from the price.

"Christopher, oysters are so yummy; would you mind if I started with a few?" Winnie said, speaking in baby talk that turns me off big time, but I nodded in agreement. Our server delivered Winnie's third Mojito in a glass I could have used to wash out my socks and took our order.

"I'll have a dozen oysters," Miss Ritz said, overwhelming me with her greed since the puny mollusks went for three dollars each. "Then we're going to split the rack of lamb, medium-rare, please."

I preferred lamb medium-well, but let it pass.

"I'll start with a small green salad," I said, praying they had such an item as it wasn't listed on the menu.

"Ooh," Baby Snooks crooned, "a salad! What a good idea; I'll have one after the oysters, but make mine a Caesar." A four-teen-dollar Caesar. Even Julius didn't spend that much on a salad.

Winnie was pretty in an offbeat sort of way; her eyes were deeply set and her nose a bit long and somewhat pointed, giving her the appearance of a wolf or a wild dog. She was in great shape, probably from working out, which is something I've been meaning to do.

When the lamb was presented it looked like a raw wound and Winnie immediately commandeered the situation and sent it back. Our waiter couldn't have been nicer, and whisked it away for more time on the grill. Ten minutes later a new rack appeared and this one was done to perfection, even for me. The captain carved it into six tiny chops, each no bigger than your pinky, and treated me to another club soda. Wolfwoman then proceeded to pick up the first chop, and eat it like she was playing a harmonica. Up and down, back and forth; those little wolverine teeth chomping away until the bone was picked clean. She demolished a second chop in much the same way while I sat there in wonderment.

"So, Christopher, why do you think Scotty fixed us up? I mean it's obvious that we're not the same type," said my date.

I was flummoxed that she had the nerve to state what was so apparent to me; after all, I'm a very eligible bachelor, although most of the women I've met are always too busy for a second date.

"Do you like to travel?" Winnie said. "I've been all over the world because my job makes that easy for me. It's so exciting visiting new places and getting paid to check them out before my clients do. Who could ask for more?"

Winnie's face took on a glow as she continued talking about her profession and she even showed me pictures on her iPad. She seemed more relaxed (although that could have been due to the third Mojito) and her conversation actually began to sound interesting.

"I know you're a car salesman, Christopher, but what do you really enjoy? What's your passion?" she said.

"Poetry." There, I'd said it and somehow I wasn't embarrassed. "Would you like to hear something I wrote today?"

"Don't tell me you carry around poems with you?" she asked, in a flattering way.

"Always," I said, in a soft tone.

As I read her a love sonnet I could almost hear a harmonic accompaniment in the background as Winnie scaled the last chop. Her teeth glistened with the fat of the meat, and she held the bone like a baton. I put my notebook down and took a swig of club soda. It tasted crisp and clear.

"How about a sip of my drink?" I said.

"You know, that's not a bad idea," Winnie said. "I was so nervous about tonight that I went overboard on the alcohol. Why don't you let me pick up the bar bill."

Now that was music to my ears but all I said was, "Maybe on our second date. Let's order dessert."

KEEPING UP

$\mathcal{M}$y wife and I never would have retired from the circus if Harriet's younger sister hadn't died. I was Jake Jones, the strong man, an easy gig for me, and when Harriet became the bearded lady we both made pretty good dough.

I'd been a wrestling champ in high school and won a scholarship to a local university. My parents were so proud of me; I'd be the first person in the Jones family to attend college. The summer after my senior year I took a temp job with the circus passing through town. They were hiring local kids to do the grunt work. When Mr. Bradley, the owner of Bradley's Big Top Circus, took one look at my physique, he put me on for heavy lifting. Into my second week I had to fill in for Bud, the strong man, who was late for his performance because he had a penchant for spending too much time passed out in a whorehouse a couple of miles from our stake. Even though I wasn't nearly as big as Bud, it turned out that the crowd preferred a younger guy who didn't look like a derelict. When Mr. Bradley asked me to stay on full-time, I accepted. My folks were furious, throwing away a scholarship like that, but the money was decent and I was eighteen. I joined the circus.

When the circus moved on to the next city Mr. Bradley hired new locals, including a couple of runaways, Harriet and Isla Rose. They both worked as ticket takers for a couple of weeks before Isla, who hated the life, took off with Jimmy the Juggler, a talented fellow with a snarly temper. They were married within a year, and had twin boys by the next. Harriet and I were already good friends and, with her sister gone, we became even closer and fell in love.

Mr. Bradley suggested I inject steroids to pump me up and told Harriet she could upgrade her job to the bearded lady if she did the same. I wasn't crazy about the idea, but Harriet talked me into it, saying we needed the extra money if we were ever to get married. Mr. Bradley started us both on the drugs and, sure enough, six weeks after our wedding Harriet had the beginnings of a moustache and a beard. Because of the steroids, Harriet couldn't become pregnant, which was disappointing, but other than that we had no complaints.

Harriet and I enjoyed circus life and never got bored because of all the traveling around to different places in the country. Mr. Bradley provided decent living arrangements and we ate cafeteria style with other performers who'd become family to us. Compared to similar outfits, our food was tasty and nutritious. Mr. Bradley's wife insisted that healthy meals made for happy employees and because Harriet and I were on steroids, we always got an extra piece of meat and seconds on the chicken pot pie, which was a weekend staple.

Harriet's beard never bothered me; we joked about it, but it was nice and soft, and looked cute with the pink ribbon she braided through it. The day after we celebrated our tenth anniversary with each other and with the circus, Mr. Bradley gave us the news that Isla was dead. Jimmy had shot her over some imagined infidelity and he was in jail serving a life sentence. Isla had long ago appointed Harriet and me as her children's guardians—never thinking it would come to pass. We had no choice but to leave the circus, move into Isla's house, and take over the parenting of the twins, Mack and Stu.

Mr. Bradley told us how to wean ourselves off the steroids, but Harriet would have to shave in the meanwhile. Everyone chipped in to give us a going away party and they'd each contributed to a small pool of cash as a parting gift. Our boss drove Harriet and me to the train that would take us to our new life.

Mack and Stu were being looked after by an indifferent social worker from a neighborhood agency. After a brief interview, she left us with the twins who were only too happy to see their aunt and uncle. We'd visited with our nephews on and off throughout the years, so we weren't strangers to them. Being nine years old, they were able to comprehend the horror of their mother's death, along with their father's imprisonment, and were receptive to our taking care of them.

It's a year later and our family is doing fine. Harriet has a good job down at the library and I coach wrestling at the high school. I'm going to college at night and the library is letting my wife use their computer to earn her degree on-line. We adopted the boys two months ago and Mac and Stu are happy, well-adjusted little guys.

Harriet and I have made new friends and enjoy life in our village. Harriet has reconciled with her parents, who live in the same town as we do, and I talked my folks into buying a small home near ours. The two couples have become typical doting grandparents and help out with the care of our boys. My wife and I don't talk much about the circus anymore. It was a good part of our lives, but what we have now…I guess you could say we moved from the sideshow to our own big top.

KITCHEN KILL

*M*y wife is a terrible cook. Stop right there. Don't tell me about the time your wife burned a piece of bacon or left a roast in the oven too long. And please ladies, don't counter with stories of your husbands who think they can cook and end up scorching your best pan while attempting Wolfgang Puck's Fried Wild Rice. Yes, I agree such incidents can be exasperating, but they are mere culinary glitches compared to my wife Edna's gaffes.

We met on a blind date. Edna was wearing the most enormous eyeglasses I'd ever seen, making her look vulnerable and clearly out of fashion. Notwithstanding a slight lisp stemming from her pronounced overbite, I fell in love. I'd been a bachelor long enough, forty-eight years to be exact, and I'd known enough women to recognize a good-hearted one with a molten center like Edna. After our wedding, she moved into the apartment I'd inherited, a mammoth place on the Upper West side of Manhattan. It was one of those condos where you lived 'til death did you part. The main attraction for me was the professionally outfitted kitchen designed by a former tenant.

You see, I'm a caterer and have been ever since my father died. It was a lifelong dream of mine, although surely not one of his. My father, Bryce Crane, was a mean person, an attorney, not that the two necessarily go hand in hand. At his insistence I attended Harvard Law before joining his firm, where he preferred to be called by his first name. Corporate law is as dry as paper, which suited my father to perfection, and as rich as he became from his practice was as stingily as he lived. My mother, who thank God outlived him by seven years, was a lively, spirited creature. I hated him and hoped she did too.

Whenever we could, which was almost all of the time, my mother and I dined out in fine restaurants. Bryce, although cheap, never said a word solely because his own evenings were taken up with one Nicole Horner, a law clerk in her mid-twenties who worked for us. Everyone, including Mother, knew about Nicole.

My mother and I appreciated good food. Nicole would have to be content with take-out dinners ordered up to her apartment because Bryce only appeared with her in public during the day at company business lunches. She was quite attractive and before I realized she was my father's mistress, I'd actually thought about dating her myself. Nicole was smart enough to coax my father into buying a condo for her before, I imagine, consenting to have sex with him.

Securing reservations in New York's finest restaurants was a simple matter. Bryce was well known all over town, bringing clients to the best places whenever possible, that being when the firm was paying. I was rarely included in these feasts although I knew far more about food than he did. "Bring me Chicken a la King, some rice and plenty of cream gravy," he'd say to any waiter who was within earshot, "and a scotch." He'd never identify the brand because he wouldn't have known the difference, thus leaving the bartender to pour the most expensive label to crank up the bill. Bryce never left more than a twelve percent tip, but even that was overlooked because he brought in so much business.

It was quite a different story when Mother and I dined out. We delighted in ordering whatever special was created for the day and never asked for sauce on the side or a substitution. We drank the wine suggested by the sommelier, and rejoiced in tipping everyone heavily. Chefs loved us, as did the staff; they knew our family circumstances and treated us royally.

"Norman dear," Mother would say, "why don't you go into the food business instead of being a lawyer? Do something you love and something you're good at."

We'd have the same discussion at every meal with no solution until the week after Bryce died. Maître d' Leonard, of the former Oak Room at the Plaza Hotel, had stopped by the table to offer his condolences and we couldn't help but include him in our conversation.

"One of our chefs, you know Mr. Albert, left us a few weeks ago to start up a catering business," Leonard said, "and he's in desperate need of help. Norman, there must be a way you could be in business with him."

There was, and after I quit the firm of Fine, Crane & Bates, I moved into my mother's apartment and went into the catering business with Albert.

It took two years before I decided to branch out on my own. Albert and I parted company, but remained friends. There was no real competition between us as I concentrated on the popular lighter fare like Pan-Asian and Caribbean style; not the heavy French dinners, which were still the mainstay of Albert's clientele. It was Albert's idea to set up our kitchen as a catering space. With Mother's support I opened Norman's Pantry. She was my assistant and closest companion for the next seven years. I stopped all business for a week when she died.

One of my clients fixed me up with Edna. We met at Dock's, a well-known seafood restaurant with tremendous atmosphere. The hostess gave us a primo table and took our drink order. Edna asked for a Cosmopolitan, but changed all the ingredients. Although it's fallen out of favor in the last few years, I'm still a diehard Chablis fan and ordered a bottle, hoping Edna would have some with her meal. She didn't. After hearing a myriad of mouthwatering specials, she asked for pork chops. Oh, why hadn't I just done the coffee date with her? Now I was doomed to spend the next two hours with a woman who, even with the biggest spectacles on the planet, could not see her way clear to ordering fish in what was obviously and foremost a seafood restaurant.

However, as I said, there was something about Edna that made me want to take care of her, and by the time she'd gone to the ladies room I was as hooked as the sesame crusted tuna had once been before finding itself seared, seasoned, and sprawled upon my plate.

It was assumed from the start that I would do the cooking. Edna would make the occasional turkey sandwich while I was mincing garlic for a party, but nothing more complicated than that. I turned down her constant offers to help me in my business. With two experienced assistants standing by whenever I needed them, Edna would tour the city streets, leaving the three of us to whir away in the kitchen. She enjoyed going to theatre matinees, museums, and afternoon movies with her friends, and thus managed to stay out of my hair, which incidentally was always covered with a net.

It worked well for us. We loved each other. I took to marriage as the tomato takes to mozzarella. My catering business was successful enough so that Edna didn't have to work, but wanting her own career she eventually found a managerial position in a well-known exclusive stationery store.

Things were rolling along superbly until Edna decided she wanted to cook for me.

Three months later I decided to kill her and when you hear what happened, I'm sure you'll agree that no jury would have ever convicted me.

Edna's favorite dish, one that she'd eaten as a child, was a formed boneless and tasteless ham straight from a tin served with pineapple rings all of which cooked together for hours until they were beyond recognition. Accompanying this gourmet treat were other canned atrocities such as candied yams made even more cloyingly sweet with the addition of brown sugar, honey and molasses. Peas the color of dead moss were the finishing touches. Once Edna mastered this menu, again and again, she branched out into more exotic fare.

I actually thought she was getting the hang of things the evening she served artichokes as a first course. She had plated them beautifully, with lemon slices and little bowls of melted (but not clarified like I would do) butter. Edna was pleased and so was I until I realized the artichokes were raw...she simply didn't figure they had to be cooked. After taking the hard, leafy things into the kitchen where they would be steamed for the next day's luncheon party, I returned to dig into the second course. And dig I did. Sitting on the warming tray for at least three hours beforehand was a casserole of Mrs. Paul's Fish Sticks, all but screaming for a lifeguard to rescue them from drowning in Campbell's cream of something soup.

Mistakenly telling Edna how wonderful her meal was spurred her on to the next level. She invited guests to dinner, my clients to be exact, as a thank-you for their business. I'd be the laughing stock of the catering world and my following would quickly switch their loyalties to the swarm of young foodies who had sprung up all around Manhattan. Competition was already tough enough on Norman's Pantry, and more importantly, I shuddered to think of the humiliation that Edna, the love of my life, would have to endure two weeks hence. I tried to talk her out of the event to no avail. My wife was determined to cook for me.

Experimenting with recipes of her own creation the meals worsened, but a menu, which remained secretive, was finally formulated. Murder popped into my head again as the only way out.

Edna suggested I stay at Albert's place for two days before the party while she shopped, prepped and ruined otherwise perfectly good provisions. She had already cleared it with Albert who would be up in Connecticut catering a country-French style wedding. Edna wanted her meal to be a surprise for me as well as the guests, who would naturally assume I was doing the cooking. Only Albert knew the facts and offered me my old job back once Norman's Pantry went bust.

The evening of the party I returned home at five, eager for a bracing cocktail. A bartender greeted me at the door, took my coat, and handed me a glass of champagne. Although I could have used something stronger I didn't want to create a disturbance so early in the evening. That would come soon enough.

"Edna darling, I'm here! I've missed you. Shall I come help with the finishing touches?" I said, my nerves jangling.

The bartender informed me that I wasn't allowed into the kitchen as he refilled my flute. On the third dose of champagne I realized something; the house smelled wonderful, and nothing at all like canned ham.

Two hours later our living room was filled with forty business acquaintances who were thrilled to have been invited to the party. Some of my clients turned out to be customers of Edna's and she was sure to pick up a few more before the evening ended, or should I say before the food was served.

Three servers came out of the kitchen bearing silver platters of minute appetizers, barely making it past a few couples. I tried to burrow my way through the crowd to see what travesties of nauseating nibbles were being presented, but the Ruby's were in the middle of describing a Sweet Sixteen they wanted me to cater for their daughter, Loie. My ears pricked up, however, as I began to hear compliments about the appetizers. More platters had been brought out and this time I curtly excused myself and snaked a path through the hungry masses to see what Edna could have possibly come up with to induce such pleased expressions of satisfaction.

"Norman, you are a genius!" said Huck Mixon, stopping me en route, "it's about time you fancy guys came up with some real food."

I looked at his cocktail plate, once home to the finest *ceviche* and miso-glazed asparagus, which now cradled three pigs in blankets surrounded by a few miniature Swedish meatballs.

"I'm going off my diet tonight," his wife said, "I haven't seen food like this in years. I can hardly wait for the main course."

Neither could I.

Now even though I told you I didn't smell the offensive canned ham, ham it was. However, being served were gigantic Virginian versions; glazed, scored and studded with cloves surrounded by miniature fresh pineapple halves, which were scooped out and filled with homemade butternut squash puree. Canned mushy green peas had been replaced by their verdant, crisp cousins right out of the pod, accented with pearl onions and slices of Shitake mushrooms. Popovers, toppling into the mounds of whipped butter that accompanied them, were set at each place.

Well, I don't have to tell you that the evening was deemed a whopping success, even before the mile-high, glossy lemon meringue pies were brought out. I'd never seen a happier bunch of diners and my wife never looked lovelier. I proposed a toast to Edna, thanking her for creating such a superb dinner, a meal everyone was certain I had planned and prepared judging by the amount of catering proposals that came my way before the guests left.

Later that evening I asked Edna the question that had been uppermost in my mind; how did she do it?

"Come into the kitchen with me for a nightcap and I'll explain it all to you," she said, a mysterious smile on her face.

I followed Edna into the kitchen I hadn't seen for two days, and there at the counter sipping herbal tea was Albert.

"Well, Norman, what did you think of the meal?" said Albert, who apparently was not in Connecticut after all.

"Albert, what..." I couldn't finish the sentence.

"It was Edna's idea," he said. "She suggested the basics of what to serve, and I helped put it together for her. It's no secret that your business has been falling off and we wanted to do something about it. You and I both need to follow the latest trend, which is comfort food, and that's what we gave them tonight."

"This was the best thing I could think of," my sweet spouse said.

Choking back tears, I embraced Edna and then Albert. I felt my mother's spirit in the kitchen that night, the woman who had done so much to encourage and support me. How fortunate I was to have found a wife and a friend whose generosity and love equaled hers.

When I regained my composure I thanked them both for their loyalty, and as a tribute to their kitchen skills, had another slice of pie.

Kill my wife? How could I ever have had such a thought?

TOM'S STORY

*H*i, Tom Hagen here. Hardly anyone remembers that name these days, but I was *consigliere* and chief attorney to the Corleone family for many years. Vito Corleone, also known as The Don or The Godfather, and his wife took me in when I was an orphaned child. Their oldest son, Santino, or Sonny as he was called, used to play stickball with me on the streets. We were both eleven at the time (I was born in 1916, not 1911 as you may have read) and I'd run away from the orphanage figuring anything had to be better than being whapped three times a day by angry nuns. Hanging out on the Lower East Side of New York, I always found shopkeepers who had a handout for a poor skinny runt like me, as well as a lumpy cot to sleep on. I even made a few bucks sweeping streets and running numbers.

Sonny was a leader, tough and short-tempered, but the two of us had a special bond. I worshipped him (and did his homework) while he, as my protector and best friend, kept the street gangs at bay. I remember the first time he took me home to his parents' walk-up apartment. Mama was stirring tomato sauce, or gravy as they called it, and Pop was sipping red wine while reading the paper at their wobbly kitchen table. Fredo and Michael were playing in the only bedroom of the apartment and Connie was just a baby. Mama took one look at me and decided I needed a proper meal, but not before scrubbing me down with strong-smelling brown laundry soap. I didn't complain because that gravy smelled so good and right next to it sat an arsenal of meat-balls waiting to be plunged into the red ragout.

Pop shook his head in resignation; another kid was the last thing he could afford. Although Vito Corleone went on to become *capo di tutti capi*, or boss of all bosses, Mama was the head of this family. When Pop looked up at Mama, who nodded her approval, I knew I had a home.

Thankful to be taken care of and not wanting to make waves, I tried to fit into the Corleone family, but I always felt like an outsider. Pop was the only father who cared about me (my birth father was an abusive alcoholic and died young) but I never received the same affection he showed for his natural born children. Michael, considered the smartest of the kids, was jealous of me from the start and remained so for the balance of our relationship.

In order to garner attention from my new parents I became a superlative student and my high school guidance counselor convinced Pop to send me to college, assuring him that I would receive a full scholarship. He also mentioned that I'd make a first-rate attorney. After finishing my studies at New York University, I went on to Fordham Law where I graduated at the top of my class.

I always paid special attention to Connie, not that I liked her all that much, but because it pleased Pop. He'd compare her to the finest olive oil; sweet, fresh, and virginal. Everyone knew she was Sonny's sister, which kept her safe from cat-calls or groping hands from any testosterone-charged neighborhood punks. Who could have predicted the vicious mastermind she would turn into or, sadly, the negative influence she would have over my two daughters yet to be born.

While we were all in school, Pop set his mind to becoming the boss of the entire neighborhood. He had the reputation of being fair, but firm—quite a change from the previous head honcho. Remember him? Don Fanucci, the guy in the white suit who was running the streets back then? That was one of the few hits Vito Corleone ever made by himself; most of the others were commandeered by his main lieutenants, Salvatore Tessio and Peter Clemenza. Clemenza died a few years ago and I'll tell you more about Tessio later (I can let it slip that as of today, March 19, 1988, he's not dead).

I didn't take the name Corleone because Pop felt official adoption would be disrespectful to the Hagen lineage and my Irish roots. He and Mama encouraged me to marry Theresa, an Irish girl. Theresa started out as a shy, lovely young woman, but three months of marriage and living at the Corleone compound turned her into the worst kind of Mafia wife—demanding furs, jewelry, and upfront tables at the Copa; everything that never appealed to me fulfilled her newfound dreams. Divorce was out of the question; I was Catholic and Mama would've had a stroke. But here's the thing, remember all those rumors about my having an affair with Sonny's widow, Sandra? Well, they weren't just rumors. Not only did we have an affair, but we married much later on; that also ties in with the whole Tessio story, so hold on.

Sonny and Michael both had differences with me as their *consigliere*, (Michael replaced me eventually) but not as their attorney. Being so embroiled with the whole family, I was singularly skilled in getting them off every charge held against them. Remember that senate hearing when I brought in Frankie Pentangeli's brother from Italy, the guy with that crazy bowtie? How about that apology I demanded from the committee at the end! Who else would have had the nerve to pull that off? That was the first time Michael ever thanked me for anything. It almost made up for some of his nasty digs including, "Take your wife and your mistress to Las Vegas." He was guessing about the mistress thing because I'd always denied the rumors about Sandra and me. Michael didn't care one way or the other; he probably said it to embarrass me. He also knew that Sandra had gone through enough bad times. Years after Sonny was gunned down, her children were killed in a freak car accident.

Now, remember when Kay had the abortion? I was the one who found a doctor (let's call him Doctor X) who'd do it privately. I always liked Kay and couldn't deny her request, although I knew Michael would go into a rage (which he did) if he ever found out. To this day I can't believe that Kay told him the truth. Why didn't she just leave it as a miscarriage? The strange thing is that Michael never asked who the doctor was because he and Kay split up right after that. Thank God she never told Michael the name of the physician or that I was instrumental in finding him. Doctor X was so appreciative for keeping his name out of the story that it was a snap getting him to help carry out my plan.

Another piece of the puzzle involved the undertaker, Amerigo Bonasera, the mortician who fixed up Sonny for his open casket funeral. Bonasera regretted the day he'd ever asked Pop for a favor at Connie's wedding because after that, he was never able to refuse anything for the Corleones. During his bloody reign, Michael sent body after body to the undertaker thinking that he was actually doing him a favor. When word got out that Bonasera's was now a Mafia funeral parlor, respectable citizens went elsewhere to handle arrangements for their departed. Bonasera was all too anxious to cooperate with me, and he could have won an Academy award for his role.

Here's what happened, starting with Sal Tessio. After the Corleones took me in, it was Tessio (or Uncle Sally as I called him) who was my favorite. He'd bring me a candy bar, play cards with me, take me for long walks and explain the facts of life, which I pretended to be unaware of. He bought me a baseball and catcher's mitt for my thirteenth birthday and made sure I went to church. Sunday mass became an important part of my life and to this day I thank him for that.

When Michael put out the hit on him I knew he'd leave it to me. This was Michael's sly way of handing me a task I'd find personally distasteful, even though he knew I'd have a crew take care of the actual kill. When the appointed underlings, Nick Geraci and a few of his thugs, were about to take Tessio for his last ride, Tessio pleaded with me saying something like "Can't you get me off the hook?" "No way," I told him and headed back to the house.

Once inside, I looked out from the French doors and saw those goons manhandling Tessio, but what you couldn't possibly know is that a minute later I came outside again and said, "Okay boys, leave this traitor to me." I made a big show of waving a gun around and handcuffing Tessio. The boys threw him in the back seat and Nick said, "So Tom's finally going to make his bones."

"Yeah," I said, "but I'll give you guys the bonus and let you take credit because it was supposed to be your job." They were in high spirits accepting my offer and never mentioned the switch to Michael.

I drove Tessio to the airport, his passport in my pocket, and put him on the plane to Ireland to the town where my parents were born. It's a tiny berg, and the last place the family would ever look for him if they even had an inkling he was still alive. The doctor who signed Tessio's death certificate (the official cause of death was a stroke) was, of course, the same one who performed Kay's abortion.

At the mortuary, Bonasera pleaded with Michael to have a closed coffin for the service. He said that Tessio's face was mutilated beyond repair and although he was a good undertaker, he wasn't a magician. Since Tessio had no relatives who'd want to see their beloved Salvatore's face for the last time, Michael gave the go-ahead. They buried another corpse in Tessio's coffin, and Tessio opened up an Italian restaurant in Kilberry. The folks there never asked where he came from or what his background was; they just knew he baked a mean lasagna (Clemenza's recipe) and gave free meatball sandwiches to local kids if they promised to stay in school and go to church. Tessio, who became Terrence O'Connor, married Tillie Reilly, his bartender, and helped raise her three daughters.

During the summer of 1964, Theresa and I were dining out with Michael and Connie at an exclusive Long Island (no, it wasn't in Tampa as you've been told) restaurant when I had a massive heart attack. The doctor (you know who) at the next table tried to revive me and then instructed the captain to call an undertaker. According to my will, the wake only lasted for six hours and the medicine that Doctor X administered kept me unconscious the entire time. They buried a wino's body in a beautiful mahogany coffin, compliments of the Corleone family. After the service, Bonasera went to Michael. This is what he said.

"Don Corleone, I believe I have served you well, as I did your father, but I am getting old now, and have no more stomach for this industry. I'd like to retire, but cannot unless I sell my business. You're aware of my clientele; I'm not complaining mind you because they have all been very generous to me, but I'm afraid I'm going to have a hard time finding the right buyer. What shall I do, Godfather?"

Michael took up his cause with pity and purchased the mortuary for Nick Geraci. The undertaker retired to Oklahoma where his daughter and family were located and Amerigo Bonasera was finally out of the mob business.

Doctor X and his wife were also delighted to be leaving the area as I promised them. He always worried that Michael would find out that he'd been the abortionist to Kay, so he and his wife asked to be moved up to Alaska. It was some kind of a crazy dream of theirs and once they were settled, Doctor X opened up a free clinic and he and his wife enjoy ice fishing on the weekends.

Theresa, my would-be widow, married Nick Geraci. I had a good friend in the Federal government (he later started the Witness Protection Program in 1970) who arranged to have the renowned plastic surgeon, Dr. Victor Prano, give Sandra and me altered faces and then had us transplanted to the middle of nowhere; it was paradise compared to the restraints of the Corleone compound. Under our new names, we bought a bright yellow cottage that had a lovely koi pond on the property and befriended our neighbors. Sandra opened a knitting shop and I work as a volunteer helping adults learn to read. All that cash I'd squirreled away over the years will last forever.

I don't miss "the life" at all. I'm proud of the man I am today and the woman who is my wife. Naturally, I missed seeing my two daughters and Andrew, my only son. Andrew had become a priest and because Michael Corleone was his religious godfather and influential with the papacy, he'd secured a position at the Vatican for Andrew. My daughters, under the tutelage of their Aunt Connie, married mob henchmen and became part of the Corleone family. I never saw them again.

One year Sandra and I took a trip to Italy, and went to mass at Andrew's cathedral. We watched proudly as he delivered an eloquent sermon. I waited for him to give my confession and once inside the booth, without identifying myself, I asked my son for forgiveness. I listed a few general sins, but didn't go into detail. It was enough for me to hear his voice. My own son forgave his father, and said, "Dad, come back any time."

Author's note: Thomas Feargal Hagen died in the summer of 2006. His wife Sandra and dear friend Salvatore Tessio predeceased him. Tom and my uncle, Dr. Victor Prano, had agreed that "Tom's Story," as told to me, could only be published after all the main participants had passed away.

—Robyn Prano Pachino, M.D.

FIRE SALE

I never would have purchased that monster of a house if I had the slightest suspicion that Fiona Fleur was going to betray me. Oh, that wasn't her real name, of course, but beautiful women can get away with that kind of nonsense, especially when they're highly paid runway models. That's how we met, by the way, at a Prada show in Manhattan during Fashion Week.

I am Martin Corwith, an underpaid, but stylishly dressed and sophisticated executive at *La Mode*, a trade paper that keeps businesses and department stores current on all the latest trends. *La Mode* liked my G.Q. look and compared to the sloppy breed of young men in our office, they preferred that I represent them during Fashion Week. Prada models were particularly thin this year, almost like snakes, and had vacant looks in their overly made-up eyes. Their cheekbones were sharp enough to slice bread on and were so high you needed a stepladder to reach them if you were a man of normal height. Like me.

I felt myself slipping into a boredom-induced coma right before Fiona came prancing down the runway, her bright red hair falling in Botticelli-type ringlets around a pale face so magnificent that you could hear a collective gasp among the viewers. Then, as if we were the only two people in the world, she blew me a kiss.

When the show was over, I invited her to join me at the Algonquin for drinks and conversation. I knew I'd be the envy of anyone passing by, and after we were seated in the famous hotel lobby, several of the men actually stopped and stared at Fiona—almost as if they knew her. One elderly and prosperous-looking gentleman began to approach her, but Fiona waved him away as if he were a fly buzzing around her head. He hesitated and then ignored her gesture and moved toward the loveseat and cocktail table where she and I had started to get cozy.

"Well, if it isn't the famous Fiona flirt," he said, with more than a touch of rancor in his voice. "You better be careful, young man, or she'll take you for everything you're worth. I was lucky enough to get out in time. Here's my card; you may need it."

Fiona was silent and I was about to call for the manager to have this jealous fool thrown out when he turned on his heel and left.

"Who the hell was that?" she said, stunned by the intrusion. "I guess he must have seen one of my pictures in a magazine—sometimes they mention us by name, but I certainly didn't take any of his money. I don't even know the old bastard."

"That's the price of fame, sweetheart," I said, taking her hand and hoping she wouldn't mind the endearment. "Mr. Mortimor Lattimore will never bother us again," I said, reading from the card before pocketing it. One doesn't leave garbage on the table at the Algonquin.

The two of us talked for hours, but I was in love after the first five minutes. After we finished the second bottle of bubbly and a couple of small plates, she suggested we go back to my place. Fiona made decent money, but because much of it was spent on body, hair, and face upkeep, she had to share an apartment with two other roommates. By the end of the week she'd moved into my not-so-spacious Gramercy Park apartment. Fiona was perfect, although I wasn't thrilled that she smoked and took diet pills.

"All the girls take pills for energy on the runway and cigarettes cut my appetite. That's how we keep our figures, but I'm careful," she said before pulling me close to her magnificent body that my arms could wrap around twice.

Two months later she talked me into buying a huge wreck of a home in Hewlett Harbor, part of Long Island's Gold Coast, on three thickly wooded acres of land. Along with a loan and most of my savings, I was able to make the down payment, and by subletting the Gramercy apartment and doing a little moonlighting for an insurance company, I'd manage the taxes and mortgage. Luckily, the house was a foreclosure with a relatively low price, but it'd still be a stretch even with Fiona contributing when she could. The surrounding houses, each built on five or more acres, were worth far more than ours. Fiona was emphatic that we have the utmost privacy where we lived, even hinting about raising a family there. My new part-time job worked to our advantage because I'd secured a surprisingly high-coverage insurance policy with extremely affordable premiums, so at least we'd be covered if the beast collapsed around us.

Fiona seemed deliriously happy and quit her job so she could devote herself to fixing up our home. Although living on one salary created even more of a financial burden, I was delighted that she no longer needed to be addicted to the pitfalls of her career: smoking and diet pills. We were trying to get pregnant, but with the extra hours I was working to make up the deficit, our time together was limited.

You can imagine my shock several weeks later when I spied her and a young stud stretched out on the living room sofa, both of them naked, sipping cocktails, and smoking marijuana. I'd arrived home early that day wanting to surprise Fiona with a marriage proposal and a photo of the ring that I'd put on layaway and instead came across this sordid scene.

Rather than storming in to demand an explanation, (what was there to explain?) I came to my senses and called the house from my cell phone pretending that I'd be stuck in the office until late that evening.

"Fi, honey, I won't be home until at least eleven so don't wait up. I'll cancel our dinner plans with Babs and Felix. Oops, I'm losing the signal, we're breaking up..." and clicked off. I left a message on our friends' voicemail giving them a rain check using the same excuse I'd handed to Fiona.

I peered into the house again and watched as she probably related our conversation to her paramour, after which they had a quickie before he made his exit, taking the drugs and whiskey bottle with him.

I drove around the block a few times, and then crept into the house to find Fiona asleep on the sofa, her silk robe tossed aside, and a half-smoked cigarette dangling from her fingers. I knew where she kept her diet capsules and opened thirty of them. I added the contents to a smoothie mix, blending it well with fruit and vanilla flavored vodka.

"Sweetheart! Wake up! You must have been napping. You look wiped out. Here you go dear, this should refresh you," I said, covering her with the robe before offering up the lethal concoction.

"Didn't you just call to say you'd be late?" she said, rubbing her eyes before taking a long draw of the fatal potion. "Um, delicious. I'm sorry honey, I did take one diet pill and I guess it knocked me out. It won't happen again. I was so lonely here all by myself; can't you stay?"

"Wish I could, but I really must get back to the office," I said, already planning my alibi. "Now drink up, darling, that's a good girl."

Within fifteen minutes Fiona was unconscious and in an hour or two, hopefully, she'd be gone. My first thought was to call Felix later that evening. I'd ask him to run over to the house and check up on Fiona because she wasn't answering her phone and I was concerned. He and Babs would find her and contact the paramedics who upon discovering the empty pill vial, would assume it was death due to an overdose, not an uncommon event among models, even retired ones. I'd play the distraught husband once I was notified about the news that Fiona had committed suicide.

That scenario would have worked out quite well except for a couple of points; there was no assurance that Fiona would die and if she lived, I'd be in deep shit, and just as important, I'd be stuck with a dump of a house I no longer wanted. There had to be a better way to ditch the white elephant, get the insurance money, and dispose of a cheating girlfriend.

I relit Fiona's cigarette and let it fall to the carpet. No one in my office kept tabs on anyone else; we were always running in and out, so all I had to do was drive back into Manhattan and work until I received a phone call from the police. I lit another few cigarettes for good measure, and dropped them near the thin drapes. I'd be sure to mention to the police that she'd been depressed lately and that I hadn't been able to get her to quit smoking or give up her pills.

I ran out, hopped into my car, and sped down our long driveway, protected by those three wonderfully wooded acres, and headed toward the city. Smoke had begun to rise from the chimney and in this case there would definitely be fire. I'd call Lattimore & Sons Insurance, Ltd., in the morning and ask Mortimor to submit a claim.

INTERVIEW WITH A SHARK

O h, are you ready? Is the mike on? Okay then, let's go. For those of you listening to the radio broadcast, please note that I'm signing to my interpreter who's in one of those under-water cages (as if I'm going to attack him during the interview).

Good morning. For the record my name is Milton Sharkle and I am a shark. Why is your cameraman swimming away? I told you I'm not going to eat anyone. That whole thing is a crazy myth started by a shark movie, you know, the one with the sheriff who looks like he has a stick up his butt.

A little information. Sharks are the most intelligent animals in the water. Yes, I know dolphins do all that dopey spinning and jumping around, but they only do it for special food. How demeaning. Those dolphins can be trouble, believe me, but they delude you because they always look like they're smiling. Swim with the dolphins? Seriously? You're safer swimming with us because we don't, um, how shall I say this...molest you. Dol-phins don't care what sex you are; they just go for it. Degrading. Let me give you an example.

We have happy hour down here like you do on land and mostly we go to The Shark Shack. Everyone is welcome, even that old stodgy spinster, Miss Clamcake (how annoying is that name) who runs the mermaid school. I wish the mermaids would come back to the bar, but the dolphins are all over them and the bounc-ers (barracudas) had to show them out...the dolphins, that is.

The mermaids stayed the entire evening until Miss Clamcake made them leave. Oh, they are beautiful, but all mermaids live at the school and never fool around. Pity.

Mr. Sharkstein, our attorney in these matters, had to speak to the dolphins about their deviant behavior, but they just started that nonsensical squeaking and twirling. He probably put enough of a scare into them because they haven't shown up at The Shark Shack lately. I'm sure they'll return after all the fuss dies down because dolphins are too dumb to stay away from places where they're not wanted. However, sharks are hospitable creatures and happy to let bygones be bygones. Dolphins also spend a ton of money on their drink of choice: seaweed and mussel smoothies. Our bartender, Pool, overcharges them, but they don't care; dolphins have all that show money from Sea World and they become so inebriated from the beverages they leave enormous tips.

I emailed, oh yes, we have internet service down here, The Honorable Maury (he's a whale, but very small and OMG so sensitive about it) in regard to the recent dolphin activity because he's the only judge we have for assault cases. The dolphins have been found guilty over and over, but nothing ever happens to them because they all bail each other out.

Gentlemen, you know those spam emails you get about performance enhancement drugs or increasing the size of your penis? Who do you think sends those out? That's right—your flipper friends. They have absolutely no class. We tolerate them because they love being chosen for Sea World, which makes people love the ocean, blah, blah, blah. A couple of whales have been showcased over the years, but that doesn't always work out well. A shark would never stoop so low as to be a trained fish (Yes, we know you call whales and dolphins mammals, but down here we're all fish).

So, your question is: why are people afraid of us? There is no reason at all for that. As you know, sharks are almost always in motion (give me a break, we have to sleep some time) and if something or someone gets in our way, we generally have no recourse but to eat them, or crash the boat—although that's a rarity.

Let me ask you a question. Most of us who live in the water do not come up on land. Have you ever seen a fish in a shopping mall that's not in a tank? I know turtles lose their way on the beach, but there's a very nice bunch of humans who turn them around and send them back from whence they came—the ocean. So, why must you insist upon swimming way out where you don't belong, where the waves are far more dangerous than sharks, and take part in the worst offense—deep sea diving.

Sharks totally freak out when we see divers with all that scuba equipment. Usually, we simply swim away, but there's a radical Tea Party group down here with zero tolerance for divers and they attack/eat/demolish them whenever they can. They're never brought to trial because Maury (we don't have juries, only the judge) would say the sharks are only doing what comes naturally.

A word about the manatee...lovable and sweet? Hardly. They're a bunch of phonies. Manatees actually mock the very humans who spray them with nice cool water at the docks they frequent. "Oh, this one let me pet it!" or "I'm going to send money for the Adopt-a-Manatee Foundation," and then they head over to the bar (Pool makes them sit outside because it's incredible how smelly those sea cows are, not to mention cheap) to play some sort of board game, all the while making fun of the humans who adore them. Lovable and sweet? Think again.

What's that? Oh, our diet. We eat a lot of bottom crawlers—mainly shrimp and lobster that serve no other purpose. They creep along the floor of the ocean or hang out where they can be easily caught, so they're perfect shark food. No one misses them. You know those lobsters you see all plunked together in restaurant tanks? That's exactly how they stack themselves up in the ocean—no originality. And shrimp? Don't get me started except to say that they have no toilet training.

Mostly our existence here is peaceful. I may have exaggerated the dolphin situation, but that's just a minor aggravation. Be forewarned: do not buy the "no natural enemy" thing either. We all have them. Even Maury's gotten stung by those nasty jellyfish demons.

I see your cameraman (he's back in the steel bar enclosure with the interpreter, like that would save him if I had a mind to break in) is doing that rolling motion with his hands. YES, I KNOW THAT MEANS WRAP IT UP, but we haven't yet touched on many other subjects.

Oh, I see. Time for your lunch...tuna?

Enjoy.

Extras

THE HATCHING

*H*erb noticed the eggs two weeks after he moved into a large three bedroom villa in one of the adult gated communities of Boynton Beach. He'd spent an extra fifty dollars a month in dues for a premium lakeside location and had started feeding the ducks that swam there during his afternoon walks. He ignored the signs that warned residents against feeding the wildlife and no one bothered him about it.

At first he brought along some English muffins for the ducks, but after a few days realized that he was being much too extravagant. He found a thrift bakery store in the neighborhood where they sold day-old bread in giant plastic bags for a dollar or two each. The bread was perfectly good, barely past the printed expiration date, and sometimes he'd keep a loaf for himself.

The ducks got to know Herb and waddled toward him as soon as he left his front door. Herb took a break from his home computer job every day at three o'clock to go for a stroll and the ducks were always ready for him. No matter how much bread he brought along, it was never enough. They were piggish in their appetites and quacked fiercely at the smaller birds that tried to get in on the feeding.

Herb could almost get the ducks to eat out of his hand and, although he never went so far as to name them, he could tell them apart as easily as his own children, Elliot and Simon. He didn't get to see much of his two boys, young men really, since they'd moved to Seattle. Elliot said too many older people inhabited Florida for a permanent move, but that he and Simon would definitely come for a visit in the winter. That was the main reason Herb had moved to a bigger place on the lake. He wanted a room reserved for his children if they decided to spend their vacation with him. His wife had divorced him years ago and he wasn't quite sure where she lived now, but Marcia certainly wouldn't stay with him even if she did come to Florida. Herb was positive that Marcia was insane and after he learned how to work the microwave and the washing machine, he gave thanks daily that she'd left him.

Herb discovered the duck eggs on a Saturday morning. He had slept late, and went to pick up the newspaper in his driveway around ten o'clock. As soon as he stepped outside, he saw them laid out in a circle on the small square of lawn next to his front door. Twelve eggs. A dozen. He knew not to touch them, but wondered where the mother duck was. Herb wasn't sure how and when duck eggs got fertilized, but knew that was only important to the ducks, so he grabbed his paper and went back inside. An hour later he decided to check on the eggs and saw the mother duck sitting on them. He said a few soothing words to her before going back into the kitchen for a second cup of coffee.

Later that day, before his afternoon duck-feeding walk, Herb realized that the mother had been roosting all day and he thought she might be hungry. He tore up a few slices of whole wheat bread, and left them close to her nest on the ground. When he returned from feeding the others he noticed that all the bread was gone. Herb started feeding her twice a day, and cleaned up the poop she left for him on the front walk.

Herb found out that duck eggs took about four or five weeks to hatch, but that not all of the young would live. He felt certain that out of a dozen eggs, there would be at least eight ducklings.

At the end of a month the other ducks gathered near the mother duck, sitting close by like anxious relatives waiting for the doctor to announce that labor had begun. Occasionally, the mother duck would lift herself off her eggs and strut around for a few minutes, the way Herb's wife had done in the delivery room right before her contractions had gotten really bad. He fed the ducks, gently tossing out bits of the soft White Mountain bread that had been on a super-saver special at the bakery and they modestly accepted his good will.

One Monday when Herb went outside for his newspaper, the ducks and the eggs were gone. He ran back to his kitchen, snatched a few dozen hamburger rolls and hurried over to the lake. He couldn't wait to see the newborns. The ducks were swimming about, but didn't rush to him as they usually did for their feeding. Herb spotted the mother duck, her head downcast. He threw some of the food her way thinking she might carry it back to her young, but she simply gulped it down. She swam over to Herb and looked up at him. He could swear that she'd been crying, so sad were her eyes, and then he knew none of the ducklings had made it. Herb started to console her, but realized that he was the one who needed comforting.

The mother duck ate another roll, looked up at Herb as if to say, "These things happen," and swam away.

A PERFECT STRANGER

$\mathcal{S}$ eated alone at her usual bench near a small flower garden in the park, Mrs. Drayton seemed oblivious to the beautiful fall day. The instant she began working on her crossword puzzle a shadow appeared in her view. She looked up and saw a tall man standing there holding his raincoat and a briefcase.

"Do you mind if I share the bench with you?" he said.

"Well, I *am* expecting to meet a friend here shortly," she said, glancing at her watch. Although the police department had beefed up foot patrol in the park lately due to recent muggings, Mrs. Drayton was still a little nervous about this stranger joining her.

"That's fine, because I only have a few minutes to relax before moving on to my next appointment," he said.

As there was no other empty bench and with a police officer standing a few yards away, Mrs. Drayton motioned that it would be all right to take a seat. She didn't want to appear selfish; the truth was that her friend wouldn't be there for at least a half hour.

"It's perfect sitting-in-the-park weather; looks like everyone had the same idea, so please, let me move my tote bag to give you some room," she said.

He made himself comfortable on the bench and placed his leather briefcase on the ground next to him.

Leaning over, he noticed the difficult puzzle she was working on.

"My goodness, the New York Times Sunday crossword, and in ink. I'm impressed."

"Don't be, I get half the answers wrong, but it does help pass the time." she said, with a sigh.

"Don't tell me a pretty woman like you doesn't have a lot of things to keep her busy." Checking her left hand he said, "And I see you're married."

"Yes I am. I never worked after our wedding and my husband is retired. I have more time than I know what to do with," she said, twisting the diamond and emerald ring away from his view although the damage had already been done. She knew he'd gotten a glimpse of her wedding band that was worth a bundle. Once again, she was happy for the police officer standing in plain sight.

"Any kids? I hope you don't mind my asking."

"I don't mind," said Mrs. Drayton, beginning to relax and enjoy the man's company. "I have three children, but they're scattered all around the country. I only see them a few times a year."

"That must be tough on you and your husband. I'm sure you miss them. At least you're free to travel, take up hobbies, and do whatever you like, of course, if you can afford it. Oh dear, excuse me please, I didn't mean to be so forward."

"Don't worry about it. Frankly, that's exactly what I thought would happen. My husband, Harold, retired early from the restaurant business and I guess I can tell you, we're quite well off, but in case you're planning to rob me there's a policeman right over there," said Mrs. Drayton, more as a joke now that she was at ease with the stranger. "I expected that there would finally be time for a long sea cruise we always dreamed about. Harold used to promise me it would be like a second honeymoon."

"Sounds great, so what happened? Harold didn't get sick, did he?"

"Oh no, he's in perfect health," Mrs. Drayton said. "We both are."

"Then, what's the problem…if I'm not being too nosey," the man said. "If so, just tell me and we'll go back to discussing the weather."

"No, not at all. Actually it's easier to talk to strangers. I'm too embarrassed to discuss it with my friends. They're sick of me complaining and they don't know the half of it."

"Sometimes people are so judgmental. I've always found it's better not to share too much with those close to you, but I can tell your situation is a painful one," the man said.

"Yes, you're right about that. To get back to your question, Shari is the problem."

"Oh, another woman, I'm so sorry. I didn't mean to pry, and I certainly didn't mean to bring up any sore subjects, but he must be crazy cheating on such a good-looking woman."

"Thank you for saying that, but I'm no match for a twenty-five year old with pink highlights, fancy tattoos on her butt, and legs like stilts."

"Maybe Harold is going through a mid-life crisis. You know, like a phase he'll grow out of?"

The stranger seemed genuinely interested in her problems, so she continued telling him the rest of the story even though the police officer had moved further away.

"Harold is almost sixty; it's a little late for a mid-life crisis. I thought that at first, but when he spent almost fifty-five thousand dollars for a motorcycle, I knew that Shari wasn't just a passing fancy. She has her hooks into him but good. Harold didn't even like riding in a convertible before he met her. Now he sneaks out to be with her and the two of them cruise around and never bother to wear helmets."

"I can't believe a man of almost sixty would do something so dangerous."

"That's exactly what I keep harping on, but he tells me stop nagging. Then he says he garages the bike over at his friend's house, but I know for a fact it's at Shari's. The two of them go out on those bikes every weekend wearing matching black leather jackets with fringes."

"How'd you find all this out?" said the stranger.

"The easy way, I hired a private detective," Mrs. Drayton said, with pride. She and the stranger were now talking like old friends and she was almost glad that the police officer had moved on to another area of the park.

"Well," the man said, "if you have proof that Harold's committing adultery, you might be able to receive a hefty divorce settlement."

"That's what I thought until I found out this is a no-fault divorce state and I'm only entitled to half the assets from the time our marriage began. No one seems to even care about adultery anymore. Most of Harold's money was inherited several years before we ever knew each other. I'd never have enough to live on if we divorced. It'd be tough being single at my age, but to be struggling financially, I simply can't do it. So even though he's cheating on me, I don't have to worry about money as long as we're still married. I only hope Shari doesn't talk him into divorcing me."

The stranger appeared to be sympathetic and said, "I take it you don't have one of those pre-nups in your favor."

"I was very much in love with Harold and he promised we'd be married forever, so it didn't seem necessary. I stayed in love with him right up until I found out he was being unfaithful to me. Now I hardly see him anymore because he and Shari are off on the motorcycle going heaven knows where. I'm afraid we'll never go on that cruise together."

"I'm really sorry. You're such a classy lady; I wish I could do something."

"Believe it or not, you have helped just by listening. It's so good to finally get all this off my chest. It's been like a therapy session for me."

"That's not quite my line of work, but I'm happy if I've helped you. Let me understand your predicament. As long as you're married you don't have to worry about money, right?"

"Exactly, so I put up with his cheating and lying, and pray he doesn't ask for a divorce. And I have to hope that Shari doesn't talk him into that either."

"Gee, I'm afraid it doesn't sound too good for you either way. I guess there's no way out then, is there?"

"No," Mrs. Drayton said, "not unless the motorcycle breaks down and they go off the road and get themselves killed. It's a wonder the two of them are still alive. Harold's become a real daredevil. The one and only time I rode with him I was scared stiff. He goes up and down those mountains like a wild man. I wouldn't be the least bit surprised if he and Shari go right through the guard rail one of these days. No, I wouldn't be surprised at all and I don't think I'd even shed a tear after the way he's behaved."

"Well, Mrs. Drayton—it is Drayton, isn't it?" the man said, while lifting his briefcase onto his lap. He opened up the leather attaché and took out a hard cover book.

Peering at the novel he was holding Mrs. Drayton said, "Oh, I see you have the number one best seller like you said you'd bring along. Are you enjoying it, Mr. Smith?"

"Indeed I am. You know, bikers have nasty spills all the time and if they don't wear helmets, let's just say I can guarantee it would be fatal."

"Isn't it wonderful how much you can find online these days? A book, a private detective, and, of course, you. I wondered if you were Mr. Smith after we started to talk, but you were almost a half hour early and one can't be too cautious these days."

"I had to be careful as well. Sorry if I kept the conversation going a bit long, but in my line of work I have to make certain my clients really want to follow through with their plan," Mr. Smith said. "Plus you're delightful company; Harold is a fool."

"I feel funny calling you Mr. Smith—I think of us as friends, but I understand the confidential nature of your business. So, here you go," said Mrs. Drayton, pulling out an envelope from her tote bag and handing it to him. "It's all the information you'll need plus half the money. I'll have the rest for you after the funeral. At least Harold didn't have the nerve to change his will to make Shari the beneficiary. It's all for the children and me."

Mr. Smith tucked the envelope inside his briefcase and stood up.

"I hear there's going to be a terrible accident up around Eagle Mountain this Saturday. You'd better call the police first thing Sunday morning. Tell them Harold never came home and you're worried sick about him. Goodbye Mrs. Drayton, enjoy your puzzle and in a few weeks perhaps you can take a nice long singles cruise."

Mrs. Drayton watched him leave and then threw her crossword puzzle into a nearby trash can. She had better things to do with her time.

THE MEN'S CLUB

*T*hey meet every day at two. Coffee time at the donut shop—the conference room they've retired to in Florida. Men dressed in a variety of mismatched shirts and slacks wear sun-shielding caps, which they remove out of respect for the ladies sipping lattes or iced teas at the far table. Paulie, the owner and one of them, pours countless refills for free, not the usual fifty cents he charges everyone else.

The men talk of businesses sold years ago when they held power in their hands, not donuts with sugar sprinkling onto their laps. They tell tales of war, Iodine Ike, and Dr. Morphine. Memories decades old are sharp and bitter—banter only veterans understand.

Steady conversation is filled with strong opinions, familiar jokes, aches and pains, and all too often the sad news that they've lost a friend.

Always polite, they make room for any gent with lonely eyes. "Have a seat, where'd ya serve? Hey Paulie, another coffee here," which is already on its way, with a free donut for a first-timer.

The men sit till late in the day reluctant to leave their sacred circle. The lucky ones know their wives expect them home to get ready for the early bird dinners they've grown accustomed to. Widowers never decline an invitation to come along for a meal. No one is a third wheel in this fraternity.

"So long," "See ya later," "Take it easy." Anything, but good-bye. The Men's Club is adjourned, but for the price of a donut and a cup of coffee, they'll reconvene the following day.

End Story

SITTING PRETTY

*M*y father, Dr. Jim Luang, lived just long enough to say "she's pretty" after my mother gave birth to me on February 19, 1980 at Manhattan's Lenox Hill Hospital. A moment later he suffered a fatal heart attack. The next day, while my mother was still in shock, the hospital asked for a baby name.

"She's Pretty," my mother said.

"Yes, she's a beautiful baby, but we need a name for the birth certificate."

"Her father named her. Pretty."

The name was bearable when I was a toddler, and people thought it was precious when they asked for my name and I'd say, "I'm Pretty." "Yes, you certainly are," they'd respond, not having a clue that I wasn't using the word as an adjective.

By the time kindergarten rolled around I was still cute, but as my Asian features became more prominent, and not in a Lucy Liu kind of way, the name fit me less with each higher grade, particularly when I reached those awkward pre-teen years. Then I wasn't so pretty anymore, kicking off a slew of cutting remarks.

"Who says?"

"Yeah, pretty ugly, you mean," were two of the more common ones I heard all throughout middle school.

"Ma, please change my name," I said each night over dinner. "You and Aunties have such cool names; let me take your name— Aimee."

"Why? Pretty is the name your father gave you," she said. "It's his only gift to you."

"Why didn't you at least give me a middle name? Even a Chinese name. Everyone makes fun of me," I said, my pleas falling on deaf ears.

Dinner was rarely just the two of us. After my dad died, Ma's two sisters came to live with us in our apartment on Lexington and 79th Street. It was a pre-war co-op with three bedrooms that Dad originally shared with two roommates when they all interned over at Lenox Hill Hospital two short blocks away. Coincidentally, my father became a general surgeon around the same time that his roommates fell in love with each other and moved out to share their own place, leaving my dad with an enormous space that he could now afford on his own.

Dad climbed the medical and social ladder at Lenox Hill, and after my parents' fifth wedding anniversary, I was conceived. My mother worked in the pharmacology department at the hospital and was able to put in for a three-month maternity leave.

My two aunts, Joy and Cindy, Ma's younger sisters, had decided to go into business and opened a bakery located within walking distance of the hospital. My aunts, who shared a small condo in Queens, sold their apartment and moved in with us after my father's death. Although the business did well, selling baked goods couldn't cover rent on their own Manhattan apartment; even if that were possible, there was never a question about leaving Ma and me alone.

My mother was born in mainland China and was more traditional than her sisters. Joy and Cindy, as first generation Asian-Americans, decided going into business suited them better than the field they'd originally studied: communications.

"Communications is such a general term, but everyone knows what a cupcake is," said Auntie Joy. "And everyone's on the Asian bandwagon these days so we're doing green tea icing, red bean filling; everything that Auntie Cindy and I don't even like."

"That's right, Pretty," Auntie Cindy said, laughing as she always did when her sister made a joke. "We're chocoholics."

The cupcake routine went on during dinners that Ma cooked and served. My aunts asked her to help in the bakery, "Chinese Confections," but Ma said she'd rather stay home and keep house. My father had left a sizable insurance policy, but her sisters insisted upon paying what they could, so Ma put their share into a college fund for me.

Auntie Cindy told me Ma never recovered from watching her beloved husband die before he ever had a chance to hold his baby girl. Maybe that's why she had a self-imposed routine of shopping for groceries or household goods on Tuesdays and Thursdays, and visiting her favorite department store, Marigold's, on Saturdays; the discipline of those regular chores holding her together. Ma went out to lunch with her sisters on Mondays when the bakery was closed, but most of the time she stayed home where she cooked and cleaned non-stop, read two or three novels a week, and watched Lifetime movies while ironing the different colored pastel uniforms her sisters wore at the bakery.

My mother was intelligent; all three sisters had graduated from Hunter College, but she was shy and withdrawn. My aunts told me Ma didn't change all that much after Dad died and that she'd always been the quietest of the three.

Ma was also a computer whiz (the hospital was always calling for her to return to work, which she never did) and after years of shopping at Marigold's, she began to order most of our clothing from them online in between the latest John Grisham book or yet another TV movie starring an aging Patty Duke.

"How can you shop for clothing online," I'd say to her for the millionth time.

"Miss Rochelle knows my size and what looks good on me," she'd say.

Because Ma was rather picky when it came to food and couldn't inspect a head of lettuce on the computer, she continued going to the supermarket twice a week pulling a black metal wagon behind her.

"Ma," I said, meeting up with her after school, "you can have all that stuff delivered. Why are you dragging it around?"

"You want wilted vegetables? Spoiled fish? Because that's what you'll get if you wait for a delivery."

"Ma, thousands of people get food delivered every day and none of them have died yet," I said.

"Yet," she answered, and the discussion was closed.

By the time I enrolled in Hunter College, Cindy had a serious boyfriend and they planned to become engaged after I graduated. Jack Graham owned a popular café located next to the bakery and their friendship-turned-romance had blossomed over the years.

"One occasion at a time," said Auntie Cindy. "Once you've graduated, your mother can concentrate on making a wedding, but right now you have to study hard. It's not so easy to get into grad school these days."

I ignored the grad school remark because I had no intention of applying to any. "Will you bake your own wedding cake?" I said, skirting the subject.

"Nope, I want one of Sylvia Weinstock's famous creations, so the more you study, the sooner you'll graduate, and then I'll let you pick out your own bridesmaid dress."

"Very cool. What about Auntie Joy? She's so beautiful, and I know guys are all over her. What's up with that?"

Auntie Cindy checked the circumference of the living room like a SWAT team member making sure no spies were hanging out before answering in a low confidential tone.

"You know that big new customer we signed on? Mr. Mitchell down at the World Trade Center? He's more than a little interested in Joy and she did more than her share of flirting when we were there with a proposal for his weekly meetings. You should have seen her showing off our samples. 'Oh, Mr. Mitchell, please try this little cream puff, you'll love it, or maybe you'd prefer our mini-apricot Danish.' I can promise you by the time we deliver the first order he'll have been in the shop a hundred times looking for her."

Following in my mother and aunts' footsteps, I graduated from Hunter College, although with a somewhat useless degree in philosophy. There was no way I was going to get into grad school because I struggled through four years to make passing grades and if my professors weren't so fascinated by the idea of an upcoming female Chinese philosopher, for sure I would have flunked out. Since I wanted to stay in Manhattan and couldn't afford my own place for probably forever, I was content living at home.

Cindy and Jack set their wedding date for the weekend after Thanksgiving. Joy and Ty Mitchell, who'd been dating for several months, decided a double ceremony would be fun. I'd only need one bridesmaid's dress, which Ma promised could come from Vera Wang's top-notch collection, and Sylvia would only have to bake one gigantic cake.

Ma broke out of her shell with my approaching June graduation and the wedding a few months hence. She gave up shopping online and went back to Marigold's every so often, always asking me to come with her, but I was still into my grunge stage.

"Pretty, you're going to need some proper outfits for job interviews and there will be parties for your aunts; I can't have you dressed like a Sloppy Joe," she said, using one of her favorite mismatched expressions.

"Okay, Ma, I promise to go with you next time and meet the mysterious Miss Rochelle."

My mother began to help out in the bakery and sometimes went along when there was a new client meeting. Ma had a good head for business and suggested that her sisters merge the bakery with Jack's next door café. The project was completed with a minimum amount of construction and turned into an instant hot spot.

"We'll go shopping for dresses as soon as you graduate, one occasion at a time," my wise auntie said. It didn't matter which one; they both thought alike. "That gives us plenty of time. Aimee will be the matron of honor and you, my pretty Pretty, can have the dress of your dreams."

Pretty Pretty. I was hearing that a lot these days. I'd left my awkward stage behind years ago and evolved into an attractive younger version of my mother and aunts. Sometimes I felt cheated never having had a dad or even a stepfather as did many of my friends, but Ma told me she had no interest in any other man.

We were our own version of The Golden Girls. Minus Miami.

Graduation day came and went, and the next event before the double wedding was a formal engagement party for Cindy and Joy, which my mother decided to host at the World Trade Center's top floor restaurant, Windows on the World. Ma had set up an appointment with the food and beverage manager to fine tune the menu and since there was also a large order for Mr. Mitchell that day, the three sisters decided to load up their van and make the drop-off themselves instead of using a delivery service.

The meeting was called for ten in the morning, so they made sure to leave early enough to deliver the food to Mr. Mitchell's board room before going up to the restaurant.

That day was September 11, 2001 and I never saw any of them again.

When the immediate crisis passed, one of my father's former roommates called and insisted I come in to be examined for post-traumatic stress disorder. In one day I'd lost my entire family, similar to my mother's loss twenty-one years ago. Edward or "Woody" Oliver had interned with my father, but went on to do his residency in psychiatry instead of surgery. Ira Broadstein, his companion and my dad's other roommate, was also a physician, and the two shared a practice on East 80th Street.

Woody and Ira had kept in touch with Ma throughout the years and I thought of them as my uncles, which is customary in many Chinese homes, even in families as assimilated as ours. They'd been invited to the double wedding, which was to have taken place in late November.

"Pretty, come in at five today. Ira and I have already cleared our calendars. You're going to need help getting through this," Woody said.

I agreed to meet them to get it over with.

It was the last time I left the apartment for the next three years.

Once all the insurance and wills had been settled, I arranged to sell my portion of the business to Jack Graham. Cindy and Joy's wills, which they surely would have amended after their marriages, presently left everything to me. I couldn't bear to think about going back to the café or any place else. I had no needs outside the apartment.

"Pretty, please come in any time at all…with your friends, or to have a cup of coffee with me," Jack said at the memorial service. "Your aunts would have liked that and so would I."

"Yes, I promise," I said, with no intention of following through.

Because Ma had taught me so much on the computer at an early age, I was an expert by the time I turned thirteen and that knowledge was ready to serve me well now.

The first few weeks after 9/11 it seemed natural to stay close to home—like many New Yorkers did—only venturing out when we felt safe again. I never felt unsafe so there was no practical reason for me to become reclusive, yet that became my pattern. Woody and Ira called daily to either invite me over for dinner or just to chat. I made up one excuse after another for why I couldn't make it.

They stopped by the apartment on several occasions, usually unannounced, but always finding me at home. I'd order up dinner and when the conversation turned to my well-being I nodded and pretended to agree with their suggestions. Luckily, they were in the process of adopting a son, so their focus shifted from my mental health to parenting.

"Just remember, we want to keep you in our lives so you can be an aunt to Adam. We're going to be crazy busy now, but you know there's an open invitation any time you can come for dinner," Ira said, during one of their visits after the adoption went through.

On my eighteenth birthday Ma had put me on as co-signer for our checkbooks and all credit cards, so I was set up to begin ordering online. Ma was right about the produce; sometimes it wasn't the freshest, but after a couple of phone calls to the store manager the quality improved.

The solitary life I was leading didn't seem to have anything wrong with it. I wasn't happy. I wasn't sad. Friends dropped by during the first year and when that tapered off, I kept myself busy reading books and magazines. I got hooked on a couple of cooking shows and countless versions of Law & Order, but my main activity was ordering clothing.

After Ma and her sisters died I had Good Will come up and take everything except for a few handbags. Since I mainly hung out in sweats or leggings, and was also on the tall side, their style of dressing didn't fit or suit me. I had the café uniforms sent over to Jack's, all pressed and neatly folded.

A few weeks after the Good Will pick-up I clicked on Ma's favorite department store site, Marigold's. During Ma's online shopping years, I once asked why she didn't patronize Saks or Bloomingdale's, and her reply was "Miss Rochelle knows me and my style. I don't always feel like going downtown."

Downtown to most upper east-siders meant Tribeca or Chinatown, not 57th Street.

At first I only ordered casual stuff, junking my old sweats that had become tattered or stretched out. It was fun having boxes delivered by the doorman and to jazz things up, I began requesting gift wrapping on all my purchases. At first there was a minimum charge, then after awhile the service was gratis.

I moved from casual outfits to mini-skirts and skinny tops from the junior department, and then morphed into bridge sportswear before working up to some of the less expensive designer departments. Several times a week, I dolled myself up in something semi-dressy, made a snack and a pot of plum tea, and sat outside on our terrace while reading the latest best seller.

My uncles now called before visiting, so I had time to throw on a casual outfit, but with their collective keen fashion eye they'd spot it as the latest trend.

"So, Pretty, looks like you've been getting out. Love your new look," Woody said. Even my hair and nails were perfect because I'd made arrangements with a nearby salon to send up a hairdresser and manicurist whenever I called.

"Yes, I'm fine now. I know how concerned you are about me, but I'm doing great," I said, praying they wouldn't invite me over for a meal, but that ship had finally sailed. Demanding professions and taking care of a little boy occupied most of their time, so they probably weren't crazy about having dinner drop-ins.

"You wouldn't be interested in applying for the nanny position," Ira said, as a joke, but not really. Although the thought appealed to me, instead I made up a logical-sounding story.

"I already have a job. I'll tell you all about it next time."

After my uncles left that evening I opened up my laptop and saw an email from Marigold's; probably an upcoming delivery notice, but no, it was a form requesting reviews for the last three items I'd purchased. I'd always deleted those emails, but decided to take on the challenge. I had to select a username for my review account and the first thing that came to mind was my name with a little embellishment. I became Sitting Pretty.

I now spent hours a week filling out reviews not only on my current purchases, but also on my past buys. My reviews were lengthy and detailed, giving precise information regarding fit, style, and comfort. When customers indicated that these reviews were helpful I made them even more creative by incorporating my own brand of fortune-cookie philosophy: "Wear this classic white shirt for a feeling of power and others will automatically respect you" or "You will out-perform any other candidate for that important interview in this charcoal gray blazer and pencil skirt."

I began to suggest entire outfits, which wasn't actually a review or even requested, but it immediately caught on. Women were filling out replies to my reviews with "Thanks for the fashion advice" or "Do you work for the store," which was exactly what Marigold's customer service department finally got around to asking me about.

The phone call came one morning as I was about to review my latest purchase.

"Ms. Luang? This is Miss Harding from Marigold's."

"Uh, hello. Yes, this is Ms. Luang."

"Are you our Sitting Pretty?" she said.

"Yes, that's my screen name. My first name is Pretty; the Sitting part just kind of went along with it," I said.

A silence followed; then a gulp.

"Ms. Luang, you're Aimee's daughter," said my caller. "This is Rochelle Harding."

"Miss Rochelle! My mom talked about you all the time."

"Pretty, we all knew your mother and her sisters quite well. They were charming. I'm so sorry about what happened. It must have been dreadful for you. We tried to send out sympathy cards to the families involved..."

"Yes," I said, cutting her off because she was working up to a full blown sob. "I remember getting it. I'm sorry I never came into the store with my mom, but I wasn't into nice clothing then, and after...well, after 9/11 my uncles explained that I would be stressed out for a long time from the terrorist attack and maybe even more so from losing my family. I stayed close to home and then stopped going out entirely. I watched my mother order everything online for years, so it came naturally to me, and I didn't have to face the world head-on again," I said, spewing forth what would have taken months of therapy to address.

Without missing a beat, she continued.

"Well then, Pretty, I'd like to talk to you about a position here at Marigold's. Can you come in for a discussion? I don't want to say interview because in our minds we know we want you."

Come in? All the way to 57th Street and Madison Avenue? My mother's downtown? Out of my comfort zone?

"What kind of discussion?" I said, after a brief pause.

"Marigold's is one of the first department stores to have developed an on-line review program. In the beginning, it helped sales marginally and then we noticed a big jump, which we chalked up to a general increase of online shopping.

I recently hired an assistant, Pamela Enright, and she has a tremendous sense of style. Pamela brought your name to our attention saying that Marigold's had one very hip reviewer, this Sitting Pretty, whom she followed before joining our company. When customers began calling the store asking if Sitting Pretty worked for us, I assured them it was a real customer and if they read all the reviews, they'd notice that not all of them were favorable."

"Oh, I'm sorry if I offended..." I started to say.

"Don't apologize. Clients prefer honesty when ordering online, and we pride ourselves on customer service."

"I'm glad I could help," I said.

"Pretty, let me get down to business. Would you consider coming out for a position with us? I'd be happy to send a car for you and we have a lovely restaurant on the fifth floor. How about talking over lunch? Then it won't seem so formal."

Cars? Lunch? Meetings? The room began to spin as I clutched the back of my mother's favorite wing chair. Although a few die-hard friends still came up from time to time and my uncles and Jack visited when they could, now there was someone who could offer me a special connection to my mother.

"What exactly would my position be?" I said, trying not to hyperventilate.

"Creative Merchandising Manager," Rochelle said. "We'd like you to go through the store, Pamela will be thrilled to be your model, and put together outfits that would be placed on our website. We want to showcase our best sellers, and you have an innate ability to highlight what other people will buy.

You won't be writing reviews anymore—that would be self-serving for the store—but we'd like your quotes for the descriptions. You have such a nice philosophical touch and that's what people are relating to. Would you like to think it over and get back to me?" Rochelle said.

"No."

"I guess this might be overwhelming," she said, not bothering to hide the disappointment in her voice.

"No, I meant I don't need to think about it. I want to come meet you and talk about my...my position," I said, hearing a cheer go up from Ma, Joy, and Cindy.

"Whew, thank goodness! How about tomorrow? Lunch? Should I send a car?"

"Tomorrow will be fine, but not lunch; I have to make a stop before coming in," I said, scratching down a note to call Jack. "How about two o'clock?

"Two it is, and Pretty, I think this will be the right step, for both of us. I can only imagine what you must have gone through. Maybe it's time to focus on the future," Rochelle said.

After we hung up I laid out an outfit for tomorrow's meeting and then called my uncles. If they wouldn't mind a last minute dinner guest, I'd tell them all about Rochelle and Marigold's.

Bonus Novella

Reptilian

*T*wo years ago, Rhoda Daniels knew it was only a matter of time before the flirting would begin. She had seen the men checking her out at the water cooler. Rhoda kept several bottles of water in her desk, but went through it so quickly when her scales itched that she had to supplement her intake in the office lounge. The scales. The lizard-like things that covered her upper arms and back had plagued her from birth. Perfect for southeast Florida.

Oils, creams, lotions, vitamins—she'd tried them all. The doctors had no answer, and even less interest in pursuing her condition. It wasn't a *disease du jour*, and research corporations weren't looking into it because hers was the only known case on record. Stay out of the sun, they'd advised, as if she could don a French bikini and sit on the sandy shores of Delray Beach or accept an invitation to the Seagate Beach Club. She couldn't even use the communal dressing room at Loehmann's or Fox's where she purchased many of her long sleeved blouses and lightweight cardigans. Rhoda had great legs but covered them up with long skirts or trousers. No use attracting a man she could never let into her bed.

Her mother, who assumed, wrongly, that the humidity in Florida would help her daughter's condition, assured her that the right man would love her for her sweet self. Her father was reticent, but Rhoda could see the pity in his eyes.

191

As soon as she finished her college degree and an in-depth real estate course, Rhoda moved out of her parents' home at Addison Reserve Country Club, rented an apartment with their help, and started to work for Winters Realty. She dated a few times, but as soon as she noticed a man taking more than a casual interest in her, she went no further. The one time she let down her guard with someone she cared about had proved disastrous. Before that, her sexual encounters had been during her college years when she refused to take off her sweatshirt.

Men found her naturally attractive and alluring because her amber eyes were fringed with long black lashes and her wide full lips set off perfect teeth. She wore no makeup except for a light peach blush and a matching shade of lipstick. Her chestnut brown hair fell past her shoulders to cover up any scales that might peak out from her collar.

She was sure that Bob Rusk had his eye on her.

"Say Rho, how about a real drink after work today?" he said, as she approached the cooler for the third time. "Don't you want to celebrate our big sale?"

"I don't think so, but thanks anyway," she said.

"Come on, it's not a marriage proposal; just a martini or ice tea. You can't keep turning me down. We go out all the time with the office gang, but I'd rather see you alone—even if it's only this one time."

Rhoda didn't want to turn him down…again. It had been months since her last date and the only time she relented and had physical contact with a man since her college days.

A year before her date with Bob, she'd met Chaz Oakley at the Delray Beach Public Library during a political lecture given by a popular speaker. She'd arrived late and scanned the last row for a place to sit. Nearby was an attractive man about her age who smiled and gestured for her to take the empty chair next to his. After the speech, they got up to leave and he asked if she'd like to grab a latte with him.

Rhoda hesitated, but decided a cup of coffee didn't have to lead to an explanation of her scales, so they walked over to the nearby popular café, Spot. Chaz told her he'd recently moved to the area and would be looking for a permanent place to live in Boca Raton. Rhoda mentioned the firm she worked for and offered to help him in his search.

"Rhoda, I don't like mixing business with pleasure," Chaz said. "I'd like to see you again, socially. I can always find an apartment, but you and I already have something in common."

"What's that? Coffee?" Rhoda said.

"Very funny. We both like political lectures," he said. "And we've already had our first coffee date, so that's taken care of. How about dinner tonight?"

He's moving too fast for me. He seems decent enough, but why start something that can't go anywhere?

"Rhoda, What d'ya say? Dinner tonight?" he said, giving her a big smile. "Come on, I'm new in town and I need a friend to show me around."

A friend. Maybe that's all he wants. I've had other guy friends; I guess even Bob is a friend.

"I can do that," Rhoda said. "I know the area pretty well. How about something casual tonight?"

"See, that's something else we have in common because I love casual, as if you couldn't tell," he said, pointing to his shorts and tee shirt. "Tell me where and when and I'll be there, unless you want me to pick you up."

"No, let's meet over at Boston's; it's across from the ocean, right off Atlantic Avenue. You can't miss it."

"Perfect, that's why I came to Florida; I love the beach. Is eight too late for you? I want to get settled in my hotel room."

"Sure, eight's fine."

That was the start of their friendship, but after two months neither of them could deny a growing attraction for each other.

I really like this man, but how can I let him get close to me? He's been such a gentleman, sending me flowers after our first date and taking me out for dinner. He'll be repelled once he sees me undressed. Maybe with the lights off, and if I use that new body oil Mom bought for me it won't be so bad. Chaz and I are growing closer each day—he's going to want more.

Chaz did want more and when he kissed her one evening, she didn't pull back. They were on her sofa, and after almost a half hour he gently pushed her to arms length.

"Rhoda, we can't keep making out like this. It's driving me crazy. I'm like a horny teenager. Let me make love to you," Chaz said.

I have to tell him, but maybe not just yet. I'm not itching, so perhaps that new stuff helped.

Rhoda nodded, and they walked into her darkened bedroom. Chaz went over to the night table and turned on a small lamp.

"You're so beautiful. I want to see that body near mine when we make love," Chaz said, his voice husky with passion.

"Let's leave it off tonight, please. I'm shy and it's our first time. Do you mind?"

"I'd prefer to see you, but if I don't get into bed with you soon—lights on or off—I'm going to explode," he said, and started to undress.

Rhoda did the same and they both got into her queen-sized bed. She lay on her back with her arms stretched overhead, so he couldn't feel the outer part of her upper arms where the scales were the worst. She pulled the covers up to her neck, but he threw back the blanket and began to stroke her body. It wasn't long before they were fully ready for each other.

At least we're in the missionary position. He can't get to my back.

After they were both satisfied, he pulled her on top of him and began to caress her back.

"Wait! Don't..." she started to say, but it was too late.

"Jesus! What the hell..." he yelled, and tossed Rhoda on her side. "What is that?"

Chaz jumped out of bed, threw on the overhead lights and grabbed his jeans.

"Chaz, please, I was going to tell you. It's a skin condition, but it's not contagious," she said, hoping he would calm down.

"A skin condition? Acne is a skin condition! You look like a fucking reptile! I'm leaving and if you say one word that we ever got together, I'll fucking kill you!" he said, and ran out of the bedroom and her apartment with his shirt and shoes in hand.

Sorry Mom, you were wrong. No man could ever overlook my scales. Thanks for the oil.

Bob Rusk and Rhoda had worked together for two years as a real estate team for Winters Realty and their specialty was showing exclusive and expensive country club properties to wealthy clients. They'd made an arrangement early on to cover for each other when necessary and to split whatever commissions they made, minus what went to the office. Their boss, Max Winters, knew that most of the agents worked in pairs and didn't care about their deals as long as they brought in the loot and got along with the rest of the other office employees. Rhoda and Bob were consistently at the top of their game and fit in well with their co-workers.

Rhoda knew the day would come when Bob would want to take her out on a date. She closed her eyes and said one of her silent prayers.

Please let it be okay. Just once let a man not care about my scales, but I'm getting ahead of myself. It's only a drink. Yeah, like it was "only coffee." This time I'll be more careful. Not all men are as cruel as Chaz.

"So, Rho, what's the deal? You're getting that far away look in your eyes again," Bob said, after a lengthy silence from Rhoda.

"Sorry Bob, I was thinking about that new client who was in here the other day. Tonight's fine, but I can only stay for one drink, my parents are expecting me for dinner," she said, making sure of her getaway plan.

"That's why God invented cell phones," he said, "but I'll let you off the hook for dinner this time. One drink. How about Brio's over in Boca Center? Five thirty?"

"Thanks, I'll meet you there," she said.

By seven o'clock, one glass of wine had turned into three and they'd consumed a couple of appetizers from the bar menu that Brio's was famous for. Rhoda and Bob were like any other couple having fun on a date.

"You didn't really have dinner plans with your folks tonight, did you?" he said, placing his hand on hers.

"No. It's that I don't want anything to interfere with our working relationship. We've been pretty successful and we shouldn't jeopardize that," Rhoda said, not wanting to move her hand away from the warmth of his.

"Rho, it's been two years and I've been asking you out for the last six months. I like you, and it's not often that I like a woman my age in this town. You and I get along great, and I'm tired of dating those Boca babes who mainly go out with me because they think I can get them a lower price on a house they can't afford," Bob said, with a smile. "See, I make you laugh. Why'd you finally say yes tonight? I mean I'm happy you did; I'm just curious."

"We're celebrating, remember? That St. Andrews deal was our biggest sale ever. I think I'll finally be able to stop renting and maybe put a down payment on a condo in my building. Do ya happen to know a good broker?" Rhoda said, her full lips pulling back for a smile.

"You're beautiful when you're trying to be funny; but seriously, I like being with you. I want to see you again, and not because we're celebrating a sale."

Bob called for the check and walked Rhoda to her car. It was a cool evening, so when he put his arms around her to pull her close she knew he wouldn't be able to feel the scales through her navy business blazer. He kissed her firmly on the lips he'd been staring at all evening and she fell into his embrace.

"Saturday night, at seven. I'll pick you up at your place; that's the good thing about our business, I know where you live," he said.

"Okay, Bob, seven it is," she said.

"Great. I'm finally going to get to know the real you," he said, and closed her car door.

It's your funeral once you really get to know me. Unfortunately, the real me doesn't look as good as the me in this blazer.

It was almost ten by the time Rhoda arrived at her apartment, which was a block north of Atlantic Avenue in downtown Delray Beach, and said the same prayer every time she got undressed.

Please make them go away. Please let me be normal.

She dropped her clothing on the bedroom chair and seeing that her prayers went unanswered, she put on her pajamas and got into bed.

Should I give it a chance? He's always so sweet to me and I love his sense of humor. We're already friends; I'll explain it early on so he doesn't get his hopes up, or mine. Maybe I'll buy a new dress—that's the least I can do.

With that thought, Rhoda fell asleep and had a dreamless night.

The day before their date, Rhoda ran to Nordstrom's in between appointments and tried on a number of stylish short dresses. She really did have a gorgeous figure as long as she didn't buy anything sleeveless or backless, which all these dresses featured. Finally, the saleswoman, whom Rhoda wouldn't allow into the fitting room, left the last dress in her size on a hook outside the door.

"I'm leaving you alone—although I really should see those dresses on you, but some of you young girls are so modest. Anyway, I found a fabulous cream dress in the back. It's a designer piece and on sale, and exactly what you asked for. Three-quarter sleeves and a scoop neck. It's not as short as the others, but it's chic and will be wonderful with your hair. How about letting me see it when you've got it on?" the saleswoman said. "I'll be right back. Or you can ask any of the girls to get me. I'm Gloria."

As soon as Rhoda heard her walk away she opened the dressing room door and grabbed the dress off the hook, and knew instantly that it would be perfect. The lightweight silky fabric swayed around her long legs and the sleeves hit her at exactly the right point; several inches below her scales, but high enough to reveal the smooth even skin of her forearms.

"Let's see ya, honey," said Gloria, who'd come back at the right moment.

"Here I am," Rhoda said, "what do you think?"

"What do I think? I think you're the most glamorous gal in the mall. Go get your nails done and maybe some highlights and you'll be a knock out. Okay, take it off and I'll get going at the register, oh sorry, you like your privacy. You can leave it on the hook and I'll pick it up. Meet me at the counter."

"Thanks, Gloria. You've been a big help."

The next evening Bob rang her bell a few minutes before seven. He presented her with an enormous bouquet of roses and planted a kiss on her lips before she had a chance to greet him.

"Wow, look at you! Turn around and let me feast my eyes," he said, as she did a spin in the narrow foyer. "You should dress like that more often, but then I'd really be beating off the guys."

"I prefer to be more conservative in the office and with clients," she said, trying to remain serious by avoiding his compliment. "The flowers are beautiful; how did you know that pink roses were my favorite?"

"Just a lucky guess. You wanna grab a sweater or something? I noticed you usually have one with you when you're not wearing your robot blazer."

"It is not a robot blazer. It has our official logo on it, and the boss likes the free advertising," she said, not bothering to suppress a laugh this time. "And it's always freezing in restaurants down here so you're right, I'll grab a sweater."

Well into the evening they'd each had two Japanese Bourbon Sours, a specialty cocktail at the Buddha Sky Bar restaurant, and several rounds of artfully arranged sushi and a baked scallop dish. Rhoda was enjoying Bob's company and tried to keep her water consumption to a minimum, but her scales were itching something awful; perhaps it was the dress fabric. Normally she wore one hundred percent organic cotton next to her skin, but there was no telling what she'd react to.

Please don't let me have to scratch...not here, not with this wonderful man on the best evening of my life.

Again her prayers went unanswered, and she excused herself to go to the ladies room. She scratched where she could reach, but sometimes that only worsened the condition, like tonight. Rhoda gave up and walked back out to the table and into Bob's arms, unable to control her tears. He'd already paid the bill, and the other diners were too busy people-watching people who weren't crying to notice her, and without a word, Bob guided her down the stairs out onto the street.

They were silent on the walk home, but she didn't resist when he held her hand. The itching had relented, but she knew the scales would still be there. When they reached her apartment she invited him in.

At least we can still be business partners and friends. There's no way he'll be able to accept a romantic relationship with me and who could blame him?

"Bob, I'd like to talk to you and tell you something about myself that you couldn't possibly know and that you need to hear before we go any further."

And you sure as hell won't want to go further when you find out what I'm talking about.

"What is it, Rho? I saw how upset you were when we left the restaurant. What happened? Come on, spill…was there a fight in the ladies room?" he said, trying to lighten the moment.

She didn't hold back a smile, but knew she couldn't keep her secret from him anymore.

"I'll be right back," she said, and turned toward the bedroom.

He probably thinks he's going to get lucky tonight. If he only knew.

Rhoda came back out to the living room wearing only a robe, and sat down next to Bob.

"Hey, Rho—I'm not like that. I'm not expecting anything. I care about you; I want a relationship, not a one night stand."

Not saying a word she turned her back, and let her robe slip from her shoulders.

For what seemed like an eternity to Rhoda as she sat with clenched fists and eyes firmly shut, it was actually only seconds before Bob spoke.

"So you have the heartbreak of psoriasis. I kind of had a suspicion it was something like that," he said, touching her shoulders.

"It's not psoriasis, and how could you possibly have had a suspicion? I never wear anything revealing," she said.

"You're telling me, but seriously, I've been with you on enough calls and noticed that you scratch a lot when you think I'm not paying attention. I was hoping that it was me making you all hot and bothered, but honestly, I figured it was a nervous habit or a rash. I can't say that I've ever seen this type of thing before, but I'm a realtor, not a doctor."

"They're scales," Rhoda said, and took a deep breath before continuing. "And they're permanent. There's no medication and no cure."

"Scales, yeah, you know, that's what they kinda look like now that I see them up close, but you know what else I see?" he said, turning her around and pulling her robe closed. "I see the woman I knew I loved the first week we worked together. I don't care about this and like I said, I care about you. And everyone's got something."

"Bob, you can't be serious. You're not turned off?"

"Nah, come on, honey, if you don't make a big deal out of it I won't either. How's that?"

Maybe I can be loved for myself by the right man, like Mom said.

"So, were you serious about not having a one night stand," Rhoda said coyly, now that she felt more confident in herself after revealing her deep dark secret. He'd already seen the worst of her; the rest of her body was sure to turn him on. It did, and they did, and four months later Rhoda and Bob were still going strong.

After their fifth date Rhoda asked Bob to meet her parents, who were delighted to see their daughter so happy and in the company of such a lovely man. Bob had brought a bouquet to the Daniels similar to the one he'd given to Rhoda on their first date and talked to her dad at length about tennis and the stock market and complimented her mom on the dinner. The best part of the evening for Rhoda was finally seeing her dad relax in her presence. It was a wonderful day followed by a night of passion when they returned to Rhoda's apartment.

There was no policy against office romances, so after they were officially a couple it was big news for about two hours until the crew jumped on to the next best thing that was trending. Rhoda had a feeling that her boss wasn't thrilled about their new connection, but she and Bob were still two of the top sellers so there was no reason for the mild hostility she felt coming from him.

"Rhoda," Max said, catching her as she put on her blazer, preparing to leave for the day. Bob had already left to do the food shopping and pick up his cleaning before meeting her at the apartment. "Can I see you for a minute? In my office, please."

"Sure, Max," Rhoda said, taking a seat while he closed the door. "Everything okay?"

"Sales wise, fine, but I'm concerned about your relationship with Bob."

"Max, I'm very happy here, but frankly, I don't feel comfortable talking about my personal life. We keep it quiet, but neither of us wants to hide it."

"I don't mind office romances; yours wouldn't be the first, but these things don't always work out for the best. Bob's kind of a wheeler-dealer type and I wouldn't want you to get hurt," Max said.

"Max, I've worked with the guy for two years and seen him wheel and deal. He's pretty damn good at it," Rhoda said.

"That's all true, but before you started here there was another successful team, Rebecca Danvers and Jack Favell. All was well until they started dating. They had a bad break-up and couldn't work together anymore or with anyone else. The two of them made life a nightmare for everyone in the office and eventually they both left to work for other agencies. I hate to say it, but it's a good thing they quit because otherwise I would have had to fire them."

"I know you lost a lot of business when they left," Rhoda said, with a touch of sarcasm. "I've heard all the gossip."

"It's not only business around here and I think you know that. Yes, we are one of the most successful firms in Boca, but I like to think of us as a family, so I need you to be aware of the challenges your romance can face," Max said.

"Max, it's not just a romance. We're talking about getting married," Rhoda said, and rose to leave his office. "Please keep that under wraps; we haven't told anyone yet."

"Sure Rhoda. Congratulations," he said, before adding, "if you need me for anything, you have my cell. Don't hesitate. Goodnight."

"Goodnight, Max," she said, and left the office.

She was in a panic by the time she unlocked her car to drive home.

Why did I say Bob and I were getting married? We haven't even come close to discussing it. We've only been together for a few months. At least I can trust Max not to spread it around the office.

When Rhoda reached her apartment, Bob had already arrived and was preparing one of his specialty salads. Rhoda wasn't much of a cook and relied on take-out or frozen meals before she and Bob started dating.

"Hey, sugar," he said, leaning over to kiss her hello. "I thought I'd get an early start with dinner tonight. You're a little late, but nothing's hot so any time you're hungry it's ready. Cobb Salad, and I bought some of those crunchy rolls you like. How about a glass of Chardonnay?"

"Thanks, honey. Sounds great. I'll go wash up," Rhoda said, trying to calm her nerves.

How can I eat anything with those words of marriage hanging over my head? If Bob ever finds out he'll be furious and it'll be over. No other man will ever love me. I need to keep him and I think I need that glass of wine.

After dinner, they took a long stroll on Atlantic Avenue and ended up at their favorite coffee house, Spot; the place where she'd first gotten to know Chaz. It had taken her awhile to go back there after that horrible last night together, but it had been *her* place first and she doubted she'd ever see him there again. Once they were seated with their espresso, Bob set the coffees down and took her hand.

"Rho, I want us to spend the weekend at my apartment. You've only been there a few times, and I miss being on the beach. Downtown is fun, but my apartment's right on the ocean. How about it?"

"Sure, we can do that. I have some follow-up work I can bring with me while you're doing your thing and then we can barbeque."

"I'll see if the grills on the patio are free, but I want you to come *on* the beach with me. In a bathing suit. You've been in Florida for how many years now, and I'll bet you've never set foot in the ocean."

"I've been in my parents' pool, but nowhere public. You know I can't do that," Rhoda said.

"There is nothing stopping you except your vanity."

"Vanity? Is that what you call having scales like a lizard all over your body so that everyone can make fun of me?" she said, almost dropping the little cup of espresso. "I can't believe you'd even suggest that. I thought you loved me."

"That is so not fair. It's because I love you that I suggested it. Rhoda, you're luckier than most. You have a skin disease or condition or whatever you want to call it, but it's only on your back and upper arms; you have all your limbs, right? There's a guy on the beach with one arm, and no one gives a crap. He's in the water having fun, and believe me, he'd rather have scales and both arms. There're a couple of old vets who come down in those special wheelchairs, and you know what...they're damned happy they can do it. Why can't you put on a bathing suit and throw on a little cover-up. You have plenty of cotton stuff, and no one will even notice. They'll think you're just keeping your precious body out of the sun," Bob said, with an edge to his voice.

Rhoda noticed his tone and replied, "Please don't be angry with me. Maybe you're right. Let's do it. I have something that will cover the scales, and I can even keep it on in the water. But you're going to have to hold my hand in the ocean."

Bob took her hand and kissed it. "That won't be a problem. And Rho, I want to talk to you about a few other things over the weekend. First, there's someone I want you to meet. I helped her find a place before you started working for Max. I've told her all about you, and she's anxious to speak with you."

"With me, why?" Rhoda said.

"Her name is Leslie Townsend. She's a journalist."

"And why is she anxious to speak with me? I'm certainly no story for her."

There was a long pause before Bob spoke again.

"I'd like you to listen to me and not say a word until after I've told you everything; as a matter of fact, I want you to count to ten before you say anything," Bob said. "Agreed?"

Bob has opened so many doors for me. He's given real meaning to my life. I'll do whatever it is he wants—go to the beach, see what the reporter wants to talk about, and maybe if I follow his lead, I'll have a chance that he'll propose. Then those words I spoke to Max will be true. I have to make it happen. No one else would be interested in a woman who looks like me.

"Agreed."

Rhoda didn't have to count to ten after Bob finished his pitch. She was speechless. When she finally found her voice, it took all her stamina to control her wrath. Bob had taken her to Spot, where he knew she wouldn't cause a commotion. Everyone knew them in the intimate coffee house and she was still apologizing months later after her mini-scene at the Sky Bar.

"You can't be serious! Tell my story to someone I've never met and let her interview me about my condition, take pictures, and send them to every rag that publishes those…those alien stories, because that's what everyone is going to say about me. I'm shocked that you could be so heartless. Why on earth would you want me to go public? Don't you realize how much that would hurt me?"

"It's just the opposite. It can only help you and countless others with disorders that no one cares about. Will you please talk with her, off the record, and then decide? She's a reputable reporter; ask your friend Mary, she knows everyone in the business," Bob said, sipping the last of his coffee. "Why are you being so contrary? Sometimes I think you use your scales as an excuse to disagree with me or make me feel sorry for you. You've been doing enough of that lately."

"What are you talking about? When's the last time we didn't do things your way?"

"How about when we were showing that house over at Bocaire Country Club and you practically called me an idiot because I wasn't sure about the size of the pool," he said, letting her hand drop on the table.

"Bob, there's something else going on here. We've been the best partners for the last two years; you're the first to joke around if I get something wrong. Remember the time I didn't know how to turn on the lights over at that McMansion in Boca Woods? You practically scolded me in front of the client, but I laughed it off. I certainly don't remember calling you an idiot," Rhoda said, her scales rising to their full fury even as she tried in vain to keep her voice down.

"Well, maybe I got that wrong, but I remember being embarrassed and the buyers were also," Bob said.

"They must have gotten over it because they made a bid on the house; they're probably doing laps in the pool right now," Rhoda said, holding her own without getting angry again.

"Aw, honey, let's not fight. It'll only be a little conversation with Leslie. Absolutely check out her reputation with Mary. Even if she hasn't met her personally I'm sure she knows of her."

"I'll think about it," Rhoda said, not wanting to displease her boyfriend. She couldn't take a chance he'd break up with her over a disagreement, particularly since she'd told Max they were getting married. "Hey, what else did you want to talk about; you said there were a few things," Rhoda said, trying to ease the tension she felt building between them.

"I'm not so sure it's the right time. We have to be on the same page with our feelings," Bob said.

"Oh, stop pouting, you big baby! We love each other, come on, you can't expect that we're going to agree on every single little point," she said, taking a chance being lighthearted.

Bob laughed and took her hand again, holding it close to his chest.

"Okay, you're right. One of the reasons I want to spend the weekend at my place is because my mom and dad are coming down for a couple of weeks. I have a sofa bed in the second bedroom; it'll be a little cramped, but they've done it before. Rho honey, I'm not asking you to be a maid or anything, but could you help make the living room a little more presentable? I want them to meet you, and if your parents are free, I'd like us all to go out for dinner during the week. My treat."

"So, it's meet the parents, huh? And, of course I'll help you spruce up the place—maybe add a few throw pillows or plants. Any special reason they're coming down?"

"Yes." Bob said.

Rhoda was finding it difficult to keep her composure because she knew this was a big event for Bob. When she'd questioned him about meeting his folks, he'd told her that it would happen at the right time. She hadn't pressed him for details then, but now something seemed to be holding him back from finishing what he'd started. She needed to find out what was going on.

"Sweetheart, you know, I guess I could speak to that journalist over the weekend if it's that important to you," Rhoda said, in an attempt to soften him up even though she was going against her initial feelings.

"You will? That's so cool of you, babe. I know it's a hurdle but you'll see, it won't be such a big deal. No one's going to force you to go public if you don't want to, even though you'd be helping countless others. Have a private conversation with Leslie. I won't even sit in, so it'll only be you two girls."

"I want to make you happy, Bob."

"You do. Thank you, my angel," he said.

"Be sure to let me know when your folks will be here and I'll tell my parents. Dad will want us to come to the club for dinner," Rhoda said.

"Then he'll end up paying, but it really would make a great impression on my folks. I want it to be a special evening."

"Special?" Rhoda was ready to push the envelope on their discussion.

"Well, I was going to wait for the weekend, but I don't want this to get lost in the sand," Bob said, as he pulled out a small blue velvet box and opened it. Set in white satin was a diamond engagement ring. "Rhoda, since we come here all the time, what better place is there to ask you to marry me?"

All bad memories of Chaz disappeared as he slipped the ring on her finger. She was speechless for the second time in the evening.

My dreams are coming true with the man who loves me for me!

"You kind of nodded, so I guess that means yes," he said, and laughed.

She hugged him close and again the tears flowed; this time out of happiness even though her scales were acting up.

"Hey, guess what everyone! My girlfriend just agreed to marry me!" Bob called out for all to hear. The patrons, mostly young people on their computers or smart phones, looked up, and after a few cheers and words of congratulations, they went back to their social networking.

"Let's go home, honey," Bob said. "I want to make sure that my folks can come and I know you're dying to call your mom and your girlfriends."

I wonder if he still would have proposed if I refused to meet Leslie. Why is that so important to him? And why does he have to confirm his parents' visit? He already said they were coming. And why did his laughter sound a little hollow before? Stop! Stop this craziness, and be happy that one of my prayers is being answered. I'm going to get married and when I show Max this ring and tell everyone else in the office, they're going to be thrilled for us.

On Friday, Rhoda left the office early to get ready for the weekend at Bob's condo. She found a one-piece bathing suit and a short white cotton shirt that would hide her scales, even if it got wet, and threw it into her overnight bag along with a few other items, and waited for her fiancé in the lobby.

"Hi, babe," he said, when she got into the car. "How 'bout stopping at Boston's? We can eat first and then drive down A1A."

Rhoda hadn't been back to Boston's since her last dinner date with Chaz, but didn't feel like explaining that to Bob, who knew nothing about him. She'd never be able to tell him about the dreadful bedroom scene she'd had with Chaz; she hadn't even told Mary, her best friend. Rhoda was too damned embarrassed to ever let anyone know about it.

"Or, Luna Rosa?" Bob said. "You like that place, right?"

"Great. Let's do that instead," Rhoda said, as she breathed a sigh of relief.

After dinner they took a leisurely drive down to his condo and she unpacked her bag. They made love, and aside from a late night phone call that woke her, they slept until ten the next morning.

"Who calls you at one in the morning?" Rhoda said over breakfast.

"My folks. They always forget the time difference. It's three hours earlier in Arizona," Bob said, as he cleared the dishes.

"Arizona?" Rhoda said. "I thought they were in New Jersey."

"Yeah, but not in the winter. They're out in Scottsdale for a few months."

"Oh, you never mentioned that. Why'd they call?"

"What is this? A third degree over a phone call? They can't come down this weekend. I was going to tell you later."

"Sorry honey. Didn't mean to grill you. I'll call my mom and tell her to cancel the club for dinner tomorrow night," Rhoda said, not hiding the disappointment in her voice. Her parents were thrilled about the engagement and were looking forward to meeting their future in-laws.

"Let's go. Leslie will probably be on the beach already and I know she's anxious to get started," Bob said, checking his watch.

"I was hoping you'd forget about that. Do I really have to talk with her?"

"I don't believe you. Do you know what I went through to set this up? Leslie is a top-notch reporter and doesn't have time to waste on people canceling at the last minute," he said.

"It's Saturday. I don't think she works on the weekends."

"Hey! We work some weekends, so what makes you the genius of all work schedules? Do you have some inner voices telling you about Leslie's timetable?" he said, slamming shut the dishwasher door.

This time Rhoda's tears were from fear. Bob had never spoken to her so harshly before. She couldn't risk it. She had to pull herself together even if it meant talking to Leslie when she had absolutely no desire to do so. She had to satisfy his demands before he changed his mind about marrying her.

"I'm sorry, Bob. I'm just nervous. Cut me some slack, huh, sweetheart? Forgive me?"

"Of course, I forgive you. I didn't mean to lose my temper. You know I love you, but those throw pillows you bought are hideous—would you mind returning them? Come on, grab your top and let's head down to the ocean. We'll get a couple of lounges with an umbrella and after your interview I'm dragging you into the ocean—my own personal mermaid," he said, and gave her a quick kiss. "Hey, will you do me a favor before I forget? I need you to sign off that any further interviews have to be set up by me. I don't want Leslie hounding you after today. I can handle her."

Rhoda was about to object to signing something she hadn't carefully read when he came up behind her, his hands exploring her body.

"I'm going to drive you crazy later," he murmured into her ear. "Let's get moving because the sooner we get all this done, the sooner I can make mad, wild love to my mermaid who's going to be my wife."

The beach was beautiful and the attendant set them up on two comfortable chaises and handed them towels. The umbrella provided plenty of shade, but Rhoda spread lotion on the areas that were likely to get too much sun. She noticed a couple applying sunscreen on each other's backs and sighed. Bob had trotted off as soon as they were settled to find Leslie. Rhoda stretched out, and made sure the sleeves of her blouse covered her scales. She closed her eyes, and again prayed that all would go well this weekend. It was critical that they got along and that she didn't start any arguments. She looked at the engagement ring, which didn't seem to shine as brightly as it did when he first gave it to her.

Rhoda peered down to the ocean, blue and inviting, and saw Bob talking to another man. Probably a friend from the building, yet he looked vaguely familiar. It was difficult to see his face because it was blocked by the red cap he wore. After a second glance she thought perhaps she'd met him at one of the wine and cheese get-togethers the condo put on for its residents every Sunday evening. She and Bob went to those little parties quite frequently, even on the weekends they didn't spend in his apartment. Rhoda was always amazed at how sociable he was, going out of his way to chat with newcomers in the building. She couldn't possibly remember everyone he'd introduced her to.

Wait a minute, Leslie is a man's name also. What if that guy is Leslie? Bob wouldn't do that to me; I simply won't be interviewed by a man. But it can't be; I already googled her although there was no picture. Why didn't I call Mary back? What if Leslie Townsend is a pen name for a man? And if it's not Leslie, then why didn't Bob invite her to one of the Sunday parties, so we could have gotten to know each other before the interview? Please let him be one of the guys from the building. I can't afford another blow-out with Bob.

Just as Rhoda's mind went into overtime with worry, Bob waved to a stunning blonde jogging along the shore. They gave each other a brief hug and then turned to walk back to where Rhoda was sitting.

Whew. That's a relief. I don't care how gorgeous she is; at least she's a she and not a he. Bob's never given me any cause to be jealous and I'm not going to turn into a shrew now. So what if he hates the throw pillows? We're engaged. That's what counts. He loves me.

"There's my girl! And here's Leslie Townsend, as promised," Bob said.

"I hear you have a story you want to tell," Leslie said, short and to the point.

"I'm going to take a dip in the ocean. I'll meet up with you in the party room after you're done," he said, and left without kissing Rhoda goodbye.

"Leslie, I'll be honest with you. I really didn't want this meeting, but Bob was insistent. He felt it would be helpful to others if they read about an abnormal skin condition, you know, so they wouldn't feel so alone."

"He's right. You need to share with the world, but let's begin with me. Do you mind if we go up to the apartment for the interview? We'll have to be inside for the photos anyway. Bob loves the water; he'll be in there till we drag him out," Leslie said.

Photos! How am I going to get out of that? Bob will have a fit if I renege on my promise.

"Leslie, I don't want you to use my real name or show pictures of my face. If this gets around I'll be the laughing stock of Boca, and it could jeopardize my career if clients read about it. They'll think it's catching or something. Please promise me that."

"I'm a professional journalist. I keep my promises and never reveal my sources. Let's get started," Leslie said.

"I might as well be totally honest. Hope you don't mind, but I Googled you, and I left a message with my friend, Mary Boyle, about you also."

"No problem. I expect people to do that. I know Mary, she does food and theatre reviews. So, how'd I make out?" Leslie asked.

"You have a stellar reputation, like Bob said. I wanted to ask you something; I noticed you don't post any photos of yourself, any reason for that?"

"Big reason. Some of my stories are very controversial and I don't need the bad guys throwing darts at me. And if you've noticed, Mary doesn't show her face in the paper either; otherwise the restaurants would be giving her special treatment. Rhoda, you're one of the good guys, but I still can't have people identifying me. It'll be a terrific scoop," Leslie said.

Rhoda was pleased that they finished the interview and photo session in a little less than two hours. True to her word, Leslie only shot pictures of her back and upper arms. There'd be no way of anyone discovering her identity.

"Now that we're finished with our meeting, I feel pretty good about it. Frankly, I doubted my fiancé's judgment on this, but I think he was right," Rhoda said, looking at her ring, which sparkled in the fluorescent light of the condo's party room where they sat waiting for Bob to join them.

"Fiancé?" she said. "Why that scoundrel, he never mentioned a word to me. Let's see, oh, that's a pretty ring—about two carats?"

"I don't know exactly. I should bring it in to be appraised, but work is crazy this time of year. I'll get around to it."

"Rhoda, I want to thank you for agreeing to this assignment. I'll be working over the weekend and will submit it next week. I'm sure the magazine will run it."

"You know, I forgot to ask—which one is it?"

"*South Florida Health and Science.* It's mainly by subscription, but the Argosy Book Store in Mizner Park carries it. It's a prominent magazine in the medical world, small circulation, but every once in a while they like to run an offbeat story like this to attract new readers. When I first pitched the article to Mr. Cadell, he's the publisher, I wasn't sure he'd approve, but I assured him it was all on the up and up."

"I appreciate that you respected my privacy, just like Bob said you would. I can't believe how angry I got at him for even suggesting it. Now that we're engaged I want to make sure everything goes smoothly. Thanks Leslie. I enjoyed this meeting even though I was dreading it up till the last minute," Rhoda said.

"There's my two ladies. How'd it go?" Bob said, as he entered the party room. "All done?"

"Yes, and it went swimmingly, if you'll pardon the pun," Leslie said.

"You are so pardoned. Can I interest you both in a little lunch? I have sandwich fixings upstairs," Bob said, "and a few black and white cookies. Those are Rhoda's favorites."

"Not for me. I want to get cracking on this article while it's still fresh in my mind. I think it's going to be sensational in the right way. Thanks, you two," Leslie said as she rose to leave. "Most magazines work a couple of months in advance, so don't expect to see this for six to eight weeks, depending on their current deadline. I'll be in touch when I hear from them."

Rhoda practically attacked Bob as soon as they entered his apartment and they made passionate love on the couch.

"Hey, what brought this on, not that I'm complaining, but you're not usually so aggressive," Bob said.

"I feel so close to you; you were right about Leslie. I never should have doubted you. The pictures are only of the…the condition, and she's calling me Jane Doe."

"You have to learn to trust me, completely. I'd never do anything to hurt you. Now, how about a veggie and provolone Panini, then I'm going to finish up some ad copy for Max. I'll drive you home if you don't want to hang out. The apartment can get a bit claustrophobic. It has the view, but not the space yours does."

"I thought I was staying here," Rhoda said, trying not to sound downcast.

"I have to get this work done, and I lost a lot of time on the beach today while you were here with Leslie. I'll make it up to you another time," he said.

"I'll hold you to that. Bob, before we leave I wanted to talk about our apartments. Do you think we should move in together? We'd save on rent, and maybe down the road find something bigger. I love Delray, but I have no objections to being in this part of Boca. We could make due in your apartment until something else came up."

"Rho, whoa, hold it. We just got engaged. We have to think this all out, see what's around and what we can afford. I assume you have a lease and I already re-signed here, so let's not lose any money jumping ahead of ourselves."

"I guess you're right, but we're at my apartment so much of the time anyway," Rhoda said, losing steam for her argument.

"Yeah, and you know, the noise of the avenue's been getting to me lately. It's a lot more peaceful here and I don't sleep that well at your place. You sleep like a log, so you don't hear me get up a few times every night," he said, putting an end to the discussion. "Come on, let's eat; then I'll run you home."

"What about the barbeque tonight," Rhoda said. "I could drive back for that."

"No can do; it's already taken by a couple on the fifth floor. Their entire family is coming for dinner and they'll be using up all the grills. But I'll tell you what, let me take you home so I can finish my work and I'll pick you up later for dinner. Tramonti's?"

"Oh, I've been wanting to go there forever. Mary recently did a review and said it was fabulous. I'll call and make a reservation," Rhoda said, and went into the bedroom to start packing.

"Nah, don't bother," he said. "I'll call from the car."

"Well, we should have expected that; they're totally booked. Saturday night in season. Sorry, babe," Bob said as they drove up A1A. "If you don't mind, let me give you a rain check. I had a lot of sun today. I think I'm going to stay in tonight and chill."

"I wish we were going to spend the weekend together like we planned."

"Don't start whining, Rho. One weekend apart isn't going to kill you. Why don't you call your parents; they're probably going to the club and you can tag along," he said. "I need some *me* time."

"I'm not whining, I'm just disappointed. My parents wouldn't have made reservations at the club for tonight because we were all supposed to go tomorrow night," Rhoda said, getting in a dig which went unnoticed. "I'll call Mary; maybe she'll do something with me last minute."

"There you go. You haven't seen her in ages. I've been monopolizing all your time," he said. "Aw, I'm sorry, babe. I told you I'd make it up to you—promise. I'll call Tramonti's later and make a reservation for us another night, how's that?"

It was almost five by the time Rhoda returned home and unpacked. She took a shower using the latest bottle of body oil her mother had given her from a new shop that recently opened. Penelope Nicks, the proprietor, sold crystals, Himalayan salt lamps, specialty teas, and everything else that was supposed to be healthy or just make you feel good. According to Rhoda's mother, who didn't describe in detail her daughter's condition to anyone, Penelope thought the ingredients in the oil would soften and help any skin problem if used faithfully.

The smell of tea rose, lavender and eucalyptus filled the steamy bathroom, but aside from the delicious aroma, it didn't help relieve Rhoda's itching, which had become more pronounced on the way home. Maybe in time, like Penelope had told her mother.

Rhoda called Mary who was free for the evening. Mary knew about Rhoda's scales and told her she made too big a fuss about it, but then again, Rhoda had never shared the story about Chaz with her.

"You're in luck, Rho, because I have to review Liberty's, that new place, and David's out of town. We usually work as a team, like you and...what's his name?"

"You know damn well what my fiancé's name is and I'm going to keep saying that until my wedding day because then he'll be my husband. You're going to be my maid of honor, right?"

"Of course, I will. Let me get off the phone because our reservation is at seven. I'll stop by your place and we'll walk over. Bring a sweater 'cause our table's in the garden. And leave that awful blazer at home."

"How about a pretty shawl?"

"That's a switch. It's about time you hooked up with some stylish things. This is Florida. And Rho, it's not as bad as you think," Mary said, referring to her scales.

Rhoda skipped over the remark by telling her a little bit about the interview with Leslie and promised to fill her in at dinner.

Winters Realty was in full swing for the next couple of months. Everyone who was renting for the season wanted to buy before prices continued to rise. Rhoda and Bob had to take clients separately, not as a team, and there were times she wished he'd been at her side. He was so knowledgeable about the technical aspects of the houses while she was the expert on club facilities and floor plans.

Bob was out at Boca West Country Club showing several properties and they arranged to meet back at her apartment after five. It seemed like they spent less and less time together, mainly due to their busy schedules. Both were wiped by the end of the day and instead of his making dinner for the two of them, they'd grab a quick burger or pizza. Then he'd head back to his place telling her he needed a decent night's sleep to compensate for the workload.

Rhoda was at her desk finishing up some paperwork when Max called her into his office.

"Rhoda, have a seat. Don't look so worried, I'm not going to get into your personal life again. I wanted to congratulate you on all your sales. I know you and Bob work as a team, but you're doing fine on your own."

"Max, I've been lucky. That's all it is. I prefer working together because there's a lot Bob knows that I don't and vice versa."

"You have my cell; if you need any answers, call me. If I'm not busy I can pop over to where you're showing a house and help out," Max said.

"Thanks, I'll remember that, but I'm sure you're needed here in the office. Is that it?" she said, wanting to put an end to the conversation before he brought up her relationship with Bob.

"Yes. Have a nice evening."

Max is only trying to help, but I want to work with my fiancé, not my boss.

Eight weeks to the day, the March issue of *South Florida Health and Science* hit the stands. The Argosy Book Store sold out in an hour and the supermarkets and drugstores, which normally only stocked ten of the esoteric magazine, were begging for more issues. When Rhoda saw the advance copy that Leslie sent over she was excited and relieved. No one would know.

The cover was artful; a close up of her scales had been photographed with a blue/green lens making her back look like a mermaid, the affectionate name Bob had given her after their first night. However, across the front cover on the diagonal was one word not quite as flattering. *Reptilian.*

Notwithstanding the sensationalized title, the article was intelligent, well written, and factual. Rhoda was more than pleased.

"Leslie, I'm so grateful to you," Rhoda said when Leslie called her the day after the magazine broke.

"Hey, I'm the one who's grateful. The publisher is thrilled because we've never sold a lot in the supermarkets and this time we had to run overtime to fill the demand. Even the manager over at the mystery bookstore in Pineapple Grove called to see if I could get her some," Leslie said.

"Murder on the Beach? I thought they only sold books," Rhoda said.

"Mainly, but Joanne's a friend of mine so I got Mr. Cadell to send over a bunch," Leslie said. "Rhoda, I had to go along with the *Reptilian* thing in order to score the cover; I hope you don't mind, but it's selling like crazy and I got a very nice bonus. You and Bob can put his share into a little getaway or your wedding. When is it anyway? I hope I'm invited."

"His share?" Rhoda said.

"Yeah, didn't he mention that to you? I told him when he first asked about doing the article that I'd be in for a big bonus if it was a hit. He asked for half, you know, for setting up the whole deal. I didn't mind because I never would have met you if it weren't for him. And if I do follow-up articles, if you're willing, the money could mount up."

"No, he didn't mention it to me," Rhoda said, "probably saving it as a surprise. And, of course you'll be invited to the wedding."

Bob dropped by her apartment after work bringing with him five issues of the magazine.

"Hey sweetheart, you're famous," he said. "Oh, not you, thanks to Leslie, but your scales and your story. Aren't you happy that you agreed to it now?"

"Bob, you never mentioned that you'd be getting money from this."

"How about a hello, a kiss, or something other than another interrogation. And yes, Leslie promised me part of her bonus if she received one. Is that so wrong?"

"What's wrong is that you never mentioned it to me. We're engaged and you're keeping secrets from me."

"It wasn't a secret; I didn't want to say anything before Leslie was sure about the bucks. She sent me a check, and get this, five thousand just for setting it up. It's a nice chunk of change, but it's not going to make us rich. Let's celebrate, mermaid, I already called Tramonti's."

Mermaid. Why doesn't that sound so cute anymore?

Dinner at one of the top restaurants in town was tasteless to Rhoda. Bob was solicitous, but mentioned over and over how he'd arranged the meeting and why he was entitled to something.

"It's not every man who'd accept you the way you are," he said. "You've probably had a few bad experiences with guys who were creeped out by you."

Rhoda was silent for a moment letting the sting of his words sink in.

"Bob, you're drinking a lot tonight. That was a very hurtful comment, so I'll chalk it up to the fact that you're getting drunk."

"Who the fuck are you, my mother? Now you're counting my drinks?"

"Bob, please, be quiet. You're creating a scene."

"Oh no, I'll leave the scenes to you, plus it's so damn noisy in this place no one can hear anything. I don't even know why you wanted to come here. Oh right, your know-it-all girlfriend, who doesn't have to pay for it herself, told you to try it. So now you listen to everything Mary tells you?" Bob said, finishing his Gibson.

"Mary reviews restaurants all the time. She's a food critic. Who else should I listen to—she knows what she's talking about, and I'd appreciate it if you didn't talk about her that way," Rhoda said.

"Listen to me, Mary's right; it's a fantastic restaurant and I don't really care about the prices, but it's over the top expensive for someone who's not even eating her food. I'll tell you one damn thing, I'm taking whatever is left over, which looks like your whole meal, home with me," he said, and motioned for the check.

It was only on their way out, with Rhoda holding back tears, that they saw Max seated on the patio by himself at a small table.

"Hey you two, come have a drink with me," he said. "How was dinner?"

"Awesome, but they give you so much that Rhoda here couldn't finish it. Can you imagine asking for a doggie bag in this place?" Bob said, turning on the charm.

"Yes, Max, way too much for me," Rhoda said, pulling herself together. She couldn't give Max a clue as to her discomfort. He'd warned her about an office romance.

Stop reading so much into everything Bob does. It's obvious he's had too much to drink. Why am I making such a big deal over the bonus, after all, it's not a huge amount and Leslie kept her promises. I better let up on him before it leads to a big fight—again.

"So, how about it? A brandy or maybe a grappa?" Max said. "You're not going to let your boss sit here all by himself."

"Sure, we'll join you," Bob said, pulling up a couple of chairs.

"Thanks, Max. Coffee for me," Rhoda said.

"Same for me, please. I had a bit too much in the vodka department already," he said, taking her hand as a way of apologizing for being so rude.

The three sat for another hour discussing business and the happenings on Atlantic Avenue and then Max called for the check.

"I appreciate your company tonight. I'm usually in the office so late that I rarely have a chance to run home and start cooking. See you guys tomorrow."

They said their goodbyes and Bob walked Rhoda home.

"Aren't you coming up?" she said when they arrived.

"Not tonight, babe. Gotta prepare a few things for tomorrow. Thanks for putting up with me; I didn't mean what I said before. Any guy would be lucky to have you and if you ask me, I'd bet even our old Max thinks you're a hottie."

He kissed her goodnight leaving her alone and unhappy. His cutting remarks had taken her back to that awful night with Chaz.

Bob's wrong. I'm the lucky one. Who else would have me?

For the next two weeks her time with Bob was scarce. He told her he was working on a special project for Winters Realty and wanted to hold it in abeyance until he was able to put more effort into it.

"Bob, let's run out for coffee. Do you have time before your next appointment?" Rhoda said one day in the office.

"There's coffee right here, why go out?"

"For one thing, the coffee in this office is undrinkable and I need to talk to you in private. It's important."

They walked over to Speedy's, the sandwich shop in the same plaza as their office, and sat down with their drinks and a chocolate biscotti for Bob.

"So, mermaid, what's the deal? What's so urgent that you had to drag me out in the middle of the day when I'm showing a house over at the Polo Club in an hour."

"This won't take long. Sweetheart, we're engaged and we've hardly spent any time together lately. Shouldn't we be making plans for our wedding? My mom wants to reserve the club, if that's okay with you, but she has to give them notice. Someone canceled in June, and she wants to book us. I have to let her know right away. June is only a few months from now, and it's still the most popular month for brides."

"Aw, I'm sorry honey. You're right. But when you hear what I've been busy with you're gonna jump right out of your seat."

"Shoot. What's taken my man away from me and it better not be another woman," she said, with a big smile so he'd know she was joking. When she leaned in to kiss him, he pulled away.

"I thought you wanted to hear the news."

"I do. Go ahead," she said.

"I'm working on a website design for the office. It's bound to increase our presence online, because our virtual tours, as they stand, suck. Honey, I miss you too, but the programming is taking up more time than I expected. I promise, it'll be worth it. It's all good, and our boss is going to be so surprised."

"Max doesn't know? You're taking this on without consulting him? I'm not sure that's such a good idea," Rhoda said.

"You don't think anything I do lately is such a good idea," he said, mocking her. "Stop your whining."

"When do I have a chance to whine when I hardly see you anymore, even at the office? We haven't gone back to being a team and you're always so busy after work. When's the last time we even had dinner together?" she said, trying to keep a calm voice while her scales demanded a good scratching.

"I'll tell you when, it was at Tramonti's where it cost almost two hundred bucks and you didn't touch your meal, so why bother eating together?" he said.

"That was one night, and you were drunk and insulting. Can't we go back to eating at my place like we used to?"

"We'll do that soon babe, I promise. I know I've been a pain in the ass, but I'm drilling this program so I can get it off the ground. It's not going to take me more than two weeks and then we'll be flying high. Don't breathe a word of it to Max; he's the old dog who'll never learn a new trick. I love you, mermaid. Now let's get back to work before I ravage you right here on the table."

"I wouldn't mind a little ravaging, maybe tonight?"

"You're on. See you after work and I'll bring dinner."

"I love you, Bob. And honey, please let me know what to tell my mother. She needs to put a deposit down to hold the date."

"Sure, babe, tell her to go ahead. That's the best idea I've heard today," he said, and they rose to leave.

At least he still wants to plan the wedding. I hope he knows what he's doing with this new program. Max is doing pretty well with his present business plan.

Bob arrived promptly at six and they made love before dinner. Rhoda wore a new sheer black nightgown that she was saving for their honeymoon, but felt that their love life needed a boost. After dinner they walked over to Spot, and it seemed like old times. They held hands and he kissed her hard before he had to return home and work on his project.

Later that evening Bob sent her a text saying he had to fly out to Arizona in the morning to help his parents pack up for their move back to New Jersey. Instead of texting, she called him.

"Hi honey. You must have gotten my text. Yeah, my folks need my help and it could take a few days. They want to drive back, and guess who gets to be Mr. Chauffeur?"

"Bob, you can't be serious. You're going to leave tomorrow in the height of our selling season? Did you just find out about their plans? I thought you told me they stay in Arizona until the end of May, and it's only the beginning of March. What's going on?" she said, her scales acting up along with her anger.

"What's going on is that I'm an only child, like you, and I'm responsible for the care of my parents. Is that a crime, Ms. F.B.I. agent? What's with you lately?"

"Nothing's with me lately. Why do you jump all over me for wanting to know what's going in your life? Our life. What about your web design? I thought that couldn't wait, and we need to go to the club with my parents to make some decisions. I called Mom before, and told her to go ahead with the date."

"Yeah, sure, I said that was all fine, and I'll finish my project as soon as I get back from New Jersey. Max has lived this long without it; he can wait another two weeks. Anything else, officer?"

"As a matter of fact, there is. Whatever happened to your folks coming down here so we could meet? I'd like to get to know my in-laws before we get married."

"Don't you worry. After I settle them back in New Jersey I'll persuade them to fly down here for a weekend. We have three months before the wedding. Don't you have things to do?" he said.

"I have to give my mother our guest list. I'll leave everything else up to her if you and I can't go over there together. She has great taste and it'll give her something else to do other than wasting her time and money at Penelope's shop."

"That's the woman who gave you those creams, right? Sorry, honey, but I don't see any difference in your skin. You're still my precious mermaid," he said. "Let me go now because I have to pack. I have an early flight."

The next morning the biggest tabloid in the country, *Truth or Dare*, came out with a special edition. The entire front page was filled with two pictures in full color. On the left was a reprint of Rhoda's back and upper arms taken from Leslie's article, and on the right was a picture of a man wearing a red cap. The words splashed across both photos were, "I HAD SEX WITH RHODA DANIELS, THE REPTILE." The man was Chaz Oakley.

Rhoda had just gotten out of the shower and was applying Penelope's latest cream, which contrary to Bob's remarks had begun to help relieve some of the itching, when she heard the doorbell.

I'll bet that's Bob. Maybe he's not leaving today after all, but I can't hold it against him for wanting to help his parents. I can't wait to meet them now that we have a wedding date.

She grabbed her spa robe and ran to the door.

It was Max.

"Max, what are you doing here? It's seven thirty in the morning. Are you okay, is something wrong?" she said, tying the sash to her robe.

"I'm fine. I brought you some coffee. Can we sit down?"

"Sure, but if I'm late today, it's your fault. What have you got there? Oh, Max, don't tell me you read those scandal sheets," Rhoda said, looking at the *Truth or Dare* logo sticking out of his pocket. "Thanks for the coffee, by the way. Come on, let's sit in the kitchen."

"You're welcome. Rhoda, I want you to stay calm while I talk to you."

"Max, you're not firing me, are you? You wouldn't be cruel enough to make me live with my parents again, because that'll be my fate if I can't afford the rent here," she said, taking a sip of the much-needed wake-up coffee before sitting down.

"No, I'd never fire you. I wish all my employees were as dedicated as you are. I need you to see something before anyone else gets to you," he said, preparing to spread out a copy of *Truth or Dare* on the table. The phone rang before she had a chance to look at the paper.

"Let me grab that, it's probably Bob calling to say goodbye. He's leaving for Arizona to help his folks," she said, jumping up for the phone before Max could stop her.

It was Leslie, not Bob.

"Rhoda, you're going to hear it from someone sooner or later and I want you to know I had nothing to do with it. I was as shocked as you're going to be. What time do you leave for the office; maybe I should stop by so we can go over all this before the you-know-what hits the fan," said Leslie. "I spoke with Mary already and she wants to come up with me."

"Leslie, this is turning out to be some kind of a wacky morning. My boss is here because he didn't want me to see something without his preparing me, and now you?"

"Max, the guy you work for? He's there? Does he have a paper with him?"

"Yes, and frankly, he's the one who pays my salary so let me call you back."

"If you need me, I'm here for you. Mary, too. We're on your side," Leslie said, before hanging up.

"Max, I think you better tell me what's going on. That was a friend of mine saying something similar to what you're trying to tell me."

"It's all here; come sit down."

"The Heartbreak of Reptile Scales" was the lead article written by Chaz Oakley. There were pictures of the two of them from their dating days followed by his comments about how Rhoda led him on until he discovered that she was a reptile, or looked like one. The story went on to say how he'd wanted a monogamous relationship with her even though he had to put up with her constant nagging and domineering personality. It wasn't until he'd spent thousands of dollars on her with gifts, bouquets of pink roses, fancy dinners and the like that she acquiesced to having sex with him, a night full of such terror that he was traumatized for months.

"I've read enough," Rhoda said, frozen to her chair.

"It's despicable," Max said. "I don't know how a paper can print this except it credits *South Florida Health and Science* with the pictures."

"It's true, Max," Rhoda said, feeling defeated. "That picture is of me. The other rubbish about Chaz isn't true, and we got along fine until one night. Yes, we went out to dinner, mainly to Boston's, and he brought me pink roses a few times…wait a minute," she said remembering back to the first bouquet Bob gave her. Something was wrong, but she couldn't quite put it all together with Max sitting there.

"Rhoda, there's something else you need to see in this article. There's a website for more information, interviews and pictures. It's www.bobrusk.com."

"What? Bob doesn't have a personal website; we all use the business one," she said. "Oh God, Max, that's what he's been working on. He told me he was creating a new program for Winters Realty; he wanted to surprise you with a more modern virtual tour link, but all the while he was doing this. He and Chaz did it together. I saw them talking one day at the beach. They were down near the ocean, and I didn't recognize Chaz. I figured he was someone who lived in Bob's building. They must have been making a deal then. I don't know how they know each other; maybe they met at a social gathering and somehow Bob found out that we'd dated."

"I wouldn't be surprised," Max said.

"Please, Max, the last thing I need to hear is 'I told you so,'" Rhoda said.

"I wouldn't do that; you're suffering enough. I'm going to call my lawyer at nine and see what we can do about this. Did you ever sign a release or anything giving Bob control?"

"Of course not! How could I have ever thought he'd do something so underhanded? Oh my God, wait a minute," Rhoda said, sinking into her chair.

"What? What is it?"

"I did sign something the day Leslie Townsend interviewed me. She's the journalist who wrote the article for *South Florida Health and Science*, and that was her on the phone. She didn't know anything about this trash, and I think what I signed only said that any further interviews had to go through Bob. He didn't want me to be bothered, and frankly I had no intention of giving out any other information, once was enough, so I signed the damned thing to keep him happy. I can't believe he would do this. I'm going to call him right now."

"Don't bother. I already tried. His cell and land lines go right to voice mail and for the moment there's no way I can reach him. We're going to let the attorneys handle this."

"No Max, I don't want that. It's bad enough that the world is going to know who *Reptilian* is. I can't start lawsuits; it'll only make matters worse. I'm going to stay right here until this all blows over. I can't believe my phone isn't ringing off the hook."

"The article points out in several places that all calls or emails must go through Bob's website, and anyone who contacts you directly will be denied an interview," Max said. "How considerate. If I know Bob, he's probably getting in touch with every magazine and tabloid if they haven't already gone to his website. Rhoda, you can't become a hermit. The sooner you face the world the sooner you can put this behind you. My advice as your friend is to get dressed and let's go out for breakfast. People will read whatever garbage is put in front of them if they feel like it, but your friends will still be your friends. If you make light of it, it won't be a big deal."

"Make light of something that's plagued me for all of my twenty-five years? Would you care to see what everyone's going to be talking about?" Rhoda turned and dropped her robe much as she'd done the first night with Bob. "There you have it: 'The Heartbreak of Reptile Scales.' Couldn't have said it better myself."

"Rhoda, you're not exactly an alligator. Do you mind if I touch your back?"

"Go ahead. I might be a little greasy from my mother's latest product that she bought from her psychic healer friend. Oh no! My mother's putting down a deposit today at their club for my wedding. I have to call her."

"You didn't get the cream on all of the area, let me spread it around," he said, ignoring her alarm, and with a gentle massaging motion he rubbed the lotion into Rhoda's scales. She sighed because it felt so good, and it was something that Bob never offered to do. "There, all done. Now, call your mom, get dressed, and we're going out for breakfast. I like The Green Owl and if you hustle, maybe we can get a table outside."

"You're kidding. You expect me to show my face on the street? That paper's in at least a dozen places downtown. It'll be awful."

"I'll make it better. I promise. Please get ready and we'll go."

What is it about this man that makes me believe him?

"Give me five minutes to get dressed," she said, and went into the bedroom to change and call her mother.

They had a quiet breakfast of French toast, juice, and more coffee, and no one at The Green Owl paid any attention to them. Mostly, the patrons were reading The Sun Sentinel or The Pineapple—the monthly free Delray Beach paper.

"More coffee, folks?" said their server.

"Just the check please," Max said. "We have to get to work, but let me have a dozen each of some assorted bagels and croissants to go. Throw in a pound of cream cheese also. Thanks."

Rhoda sighed because he'd argue anything she had to say about not going in to the office.

Max called a staff meeting as soon as they arrived.

"Everyone in the conference room, please. You can bring your coffees, I have breakfast here," he said. "Okay, you guys settled? Good. We're going to talk about what some or all of you probably already know."

Max threw the paper on the large boardroom table for all to see.

"Yeah, we saw that when we stopped at Speedy's for coffee and we wouldn't have to stop there if you brought in a decent brew," said Evan, one of the top realtors. "Is that it or can we get to work?"

"I buy lousy coffee so we can help keep Speedy's in business, ever think of that?" Max said.

"Nice try, dude, but we're not buying it," said Gavin, one of the sales associates, as he helped himself to a bagel and a thick spread of cream cheese.

The rest of the staff chimed in with complaints about the office coffee, not getting enough good leads, and the rag of the paper Max had brought in, but no one said a word about Rhoda or her scales.

"Guys," Rhoda said. "Thank you. I really appreciate it."

"Sure, dude," said Gavin, who called everyone dude and somehow got away with it. "Hey Rho, how about you and me partnering up now that Bob the snake is gone…oh, no offense."

"None taken," Rhoda said, with a laugh. "If it's okay with Max I could use someone to watch my back—oh my God, I can't believe I just said that."

"Enough," said Max. "This isn't a comedy club. Back to work, and Gavin, you can team up with Rhoda or whoever else will tolerate you. Now everyone take what you want to eat and get out!"

"Good old Max," Evan said. "He sure knows how to run a meeting."

"I thought I adjourned it...and stop calling me old," Max said. "I just turned thirty-three."

"It's his white hair," one of the other agents said, and while discussing Max's hair, the bad office coffee and other non-related reptile subjects, they sauntered back to their desks to check on messages from clients.

In the late afternoon Rhoda went out on a call to Delaire Country Club with Gavin and returned to the office at closing time.

"Can I give you a ride home?" Gavin said.

"That's okay, Gavin, I need to update Rhoda on a few things if she has the time. I'll drive her home," Max said.

"Sure, Max. Thanks anyway, Gavin. I think we did pretty well today. Mrs. Valdez wants to revisit the gym and spa over the weekend. I can handle that if you have something else going on."

"Sounds good. See ya, dudes," Gavin said, and after making a few notes, left for the day.

"Rhoda, I didn't have anything to discuss with you; I just wanted to make sure you're okay. How're you doing? Really."

"I had my moments today, but being busy helped a lot. Everyone in the office has been so sweet and the clients didn't seem to recognize me, but maybe they were being polite. There's nothing I can do about it for the moment. I'm sure it'll go viral, and hopefully that'll be it."

"Everyone's got such short attention spans these days it'll probably be yesterday's news before you know it. Ready to go?"

"Yes, but I have to stop at my parents'. They were so upset this morning and I want to make sure they know I'm making the best of a bad situation. They're over at Addison; would you mind dropping me there?"

Twenty minutes later they drove through the security gates of the country club and parked in the Daniels' driveway. Rhoda's father was outside waiting for her after receiving a call from the guard that she was on her way.

"Dad, hi. This is my boss, Max Winters. He was nice enough to drive me into the office today."

"How are you, sweetheart? What an awful thing that guy did. I'd like to get my hands on him," Mr. Daniels said.

"That makes two of us," Max said, as he shook Mr. Daniels's hand.

"Why don't we go in the house; your mother can give us something to drink. Max, join us please."

Later that evening, after Mrs. Daniels insisted they stay for dinner, they spoke more about the incident. It was clear that Rhoda's mother was still very distressed, but after seeing her daughter's calm demeanor, she went on to share her own news.

"I've taken a part time job at Penelope's. Just two days a week, but it'll be good for me. She's building up quite a clientele and her products are amazing. Max, since everything is out in the open now, I want to ask Rhoda a few questions, do you mind?"

"Not at all. I care a lot about your daughter and if I can help, I hope you and she will let me."

"Max, that's very sweet of you. Rhoda, Penelope wanted me to ask you if the oils or creams were helping."

"A little bit, Mom, but the oil gets all over the place. The cream is okay," Rhoda said, not adding that her scales weren't itching at present.

"Now that Penelope's seen the article, in the good magazine—not that terrible newspaper—she wants to try to concoct something that will really help. Would you agree to see her? That would be the best way. Maybe this Saturday?"

"Oh, Mom, that's so nice of you and her, but we've tried everything on the market plus all those prescriptions, I don't know if it's worth it."

"Of course, it's worth it," Max said, without being asked.

"Sweetheart, you know my arthritis kicks up when I play golf, well, Penelope gave me a salve that reduces the pain. And your mother's making us drink some kind of energy tonic in the morning. It's green and it doesn't taste so great, but it works, so please, see Penelope. We know you've been through the mill all these years; we'd like to try everything possible. If it doesn't work we won't bug you again," Mr. Daniels said.

"Okay, Daddy. I'll go over Saturday afternoon about two. I have a client in the morning. I already told my new partner I'd cover for us."

"I'll go with you," Max said. "We can have lunch with the client at the club's restaurant; that usually seals the deal. I'd like to come to Penelope's with you if you don't mind."

When Rhoda saw her mother's surprised look, she decided to come clean about her morning.

"Mom, Max saw the scales earlier today. He came over to check on me after he saw the paper. He spread the cream on my back," Rhoda said.

"I used to do that for her," her mother said. "I'm glad you were there."

"If you can get the club to give us a lunch reservation, I'll call Mrs. Valdez and tell her to meet us there at noon," Rhoda said.

"No problem. I know the managers at most of the clubs; they're receptive to our bringing in prospective buyers. I'll set it up."

"Thanks, Max," Rhoda said, and looked at her boss with mixed feelings.

Once Rhoda was back in her apartment, she checked her voice mail. She listened to calls from tabloid reporters who'd ignored Bob's instructions, and were asking her for interviews. They all mentioned that although they'd seen the Bob Rusk website, nothing further would be of any interest without Rhoda's own words and more pictures. There'd be money involved for Mr. Rusk as a finders' fee and the paper would give Rhoda a nice chunk depending on the article. She didn't return any of the calls.

Out of habit, Rhoda picked up the ringing phone. She'd have to ask for an unlisted number if these calls continued. For now, she'd tell them she wasn't giving any more interviews.

"Hello," she said, in a businesslike tone.

"Rho, honey, it's me. Please don't hang up."

It was Bob.

"If you're calling to apologize I don't care to hear it, and as a matter of fact, I don't care to hear from you at all," she said, about to hang up on him.

"Rho, please give me a chance to explain. Then if you never want to hear from me again, I promise not to bother you anymore."

"Go ahead, but make it quick."

"First, let me say that I've never stopped loving you and I still want to go through with the marriage. Your mom made the date in June, right? Anyway, I know you're angry with me, but honestly, I did it for us. *Truth or Dare* gave me fifty thousand for the scoop and there's a lot more in store. We don't have to stick with the tabloids, although they pay mucho, because *People* magazine will want us, maybe even Oprah or Dr. Oz."

"So you sold me out for fifty thousand dollars. I hope that'll last you a long time because I'm not giving any more interviews and our wedding is off," she said.

Why am I still on the phone with him? Why didn't I hang up right away? What hold does he have on me?

"Aw, Rho, don't say that; I mean about the wedding. You know how much I love you; haven't I proven that?"

"By what? Getting into bed with Chaz Oakley to come up with whatever deal you had to devise to get him to make up those lies?"

"That's only one of the things I'm sorry for. I felt really bad about that, but he's the one who first told me about you. I don't even know how it came up in conversation, but he rented a place in my building and we got to talking one day and he told me about this hot babe who would have been perfect except…well, you know the rest."

"Yes, I know the rest, and I'm sure you're sorry for only one thing; that you can't and won't make any more money from this…this mess you started."

"Rho, you have to admit that there aren't a lot of guys out there who'd want to have sex with you, much less marry you, but I'm willing to stick by you. Mermaid, we need to have a conversation, in person, because I think you're missing an opportunity to…"

231

"Bob, let me interrupt you. This is the last conversation I want to have with you. I want no part of whatever scheme you and Chaz have cooked up because the two of you may not have scales, but you're surely the lowliest creatures I've ever met. He gave you the information you needed to get close to me, but I'll bet you jerks never took into consideration that without my cooperation, there'd be no more articles or money, and your fifteen minutes of fame will be over as of today. Don't ever call here again, because if you do, I'll make sure that no one in the real estate business hires you except to sweep the floors," Rhoda said, and hung up.

Wow, where did that come from? Threatening him about his career? My doormat days are over. I'd pat my scaly back if my arms were long enough.

Rhoda knew the only story she'd ever give would be if Penelope's formulas did any good. Then she'd go to Leslie and let her write the follow-up article with pictures for *South Florida Health and Science* in case there were others who'd benefit from her ordeal. Bob wouldn't dare stop her even with his so-called contract.

Rhoda applied more healing cream on the areas she could reach and thought about how comforting it had been when Max smoothed it on for her. Instead of her long sleeved pajamas that she usually wore, she put on a sleeveless cotton nightgown. Her scales were still there, but she no longer hated them as much.

Max picked her up for their Saturday lunch at Delaire Country Club where they were meeting Mrs. Valdez, who insisted they call her Carlotta. She was impressed with the food and service and was flattered that Winters Realty's owner had joined them. After lunch they did a quick tour of the gym and Mrs. Valdez decided to stay on to speak with one of the trainers. They said their goodbyes and Max and Rhoda drove off to Penelope's. Rhoda called Gavin from the car to tell him that the sale was in the bag.

Penelope Nicks was expecting them and after the introductions, escorted Rhoda to the back room where she kept a massage table. Max busied himself looking at all the natural hair products and sniffing the aromatherapy oils. Mrs. Daniels was there to help out because Saturday was a busy day and Penelope didn't know how long her consultation with Rhoda would take.

Rhoda had removed her cotton shirt and bra, and was stretched out on the table while Penelope examined her scales and surrounding skin.

"Rhoda, certain areas are more affected than others. Did you realize that?" Penelope said.

"I can't always see what's going on with my back; I usually just check my arms."

"How long have you been using the new oils and creams your mother brought you?"

"For a few weeks, but I stopped the oil—it was too messy," Rhoda said, feeling guilty. "I can't always get the cream all over my back. My ex didn't want to do it," she continued, remembering Bob's repulsion when she'd asked him.

"That must have been a while ago because I see you're engaged," Penelope said.

"On no! I forgot to take the ring off. I am definitely not engaged. He was the one who broke the story about my scales in *Truth or Dare*," Rhoda said.

"Well then, I'm glad he's an ex. Return the ring or cash it in and use the money for something worthwhile, but don't keep it. Very bad karma."

"I don't want to see him again and I guess I could donate the money I get from selling it. I don't want any ties to him."

"I'm sure your new guy will feel better seeing you without another man's ring on your finger," Penelope said, while she smeared an ointment over Rhoda's back and arms.

"Oh, Max is just a friend. And my boss," she said.

"Let that salve work under these LED lights for fifteen minutes. I want you to relax and the herbs will do their magic. Your mother confided in me some time ago about your condition, but there wasn't a lot I could do without seeing you. I'm glad you came in today. Should I send in your friend to keep you company? I'll put a little cotton cloth over you; the lights will still penetrate."

Without waiting for a reply, Penelope grabbed a thin hand-kerchief-type of fabric and covered the areas being treated.

"I'm going to leave you now; I have to go over some of the products with your mother so she becomes more familiar with my line."

A minute later Max entered the small room and without say-ing a word, sat down next to Rhoda and took her hand.

"You don't need to keep that cloth there for me," he said. "Penelope said it was more for your comfort; it's not necessary. I've already seen your back and arms. Nothing matters to me except your happiness. Rhoda, we might not be in the most romantic place to tell you this, but I'm crazy about you with or without the scales, and I'm going to take off this engagement ring because you're not engaged anymore, or yet, and you can decide what to do with it later."

Max removed the ring and put it in Rhoda's purse. He took her hand again, and for the rest of the healing time neither said a word.

Being on my stomach has its advantages; Max can't see the big smile on my face!

After six months of daily treatments, Rhoda's scales all but disappeared. With additional monthly boosters and at-home nightly applications of herbal creams, the few leftover remnants were barely visible.

With Rhoda's consent, Leslie wrote several follow-up articles for *South Florida Health and Science,* and her publisher, Rupert Cadell, who was now her steady boyfriend, was thrilled with the growth of the magazine.

Mr. and Mrs. Daniels suggested partnering with Penelope and with their financial help she expanded her business to a full scale spa. The magazine credited Penelope with curing an unusual skin condition and she became known as the guru who developed safe natural products with strong healing effects.

With Rhoda's share of the bonus money from Leslie, which was substantial, and other contributions from the community, she created a fund for children afflicted with disfiguring skin disorders.

Bob called Rhoda one last time, and pleaded with her to cooperate with him by giving more interviews to the tabloids because the *Truth or Dare* money, which he had to split with Chaz, was running low. She refused and returned his ring.

Addison Reserve's Food and Beverage Manager returned the deposit to Mrs. Daniels, but a few months later she gave it back and they found an open date in December.

Rhoda introduced her mother and mother-in-law-to-be to Gloria, who had left Nordstrom's to become a bridal consultant at Saks. The three women agreed that the white satin strapless wedding gown was perfect for the beautiful bride.

Rhoda and Max bought a house in Woodfield Country Club, home to many young couples with children, something they found appealing.

Winters Realty is doing well. Gavin is still Rhoda's partner and still calls everyone dude. The staff continues to pick up their coffee at Speedy's because, after all, it helps keep him in business.

Acknowledgments

*M*y thanks to the Palm Beach and Broward County Libraries, the National League of American Pen Women, and Florida Writers Association for their support. Unending gratitude goes to Murder on the Beach Book Store for their hospitality. To Booklover's Bench—your guidance, patience, and boundless energy have been invaluable. Last, but never least, I credit my family and friends for making sure I didn't become a total recluse while writing this book.

Thank you for reading Sitting Pretty. If you enjoyed this story, please support the author's efforts by helping other readers find this book. Here are some suggestions for your consideration.

Write an online customer review.

Gift a copy of this book to a booklover friend.

Follow Carol: Twitter @polowhite and Facebook: Carol White Fiction

Spread the word about her work.

Suggest her titles to a local book club.

CPSIA information can be obtained at www.ICGtesting.com
Printed in the USA
LVOW05s1116010514

384021LV00001B/43/P